Fraternity of Brothers

Life of Galen, Book 1

Marina Pacheco

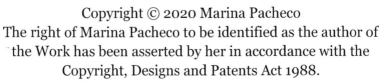

Sign up for Marina Pacheco's no-spam newsletter that only goes out when there is a new book or freebie available and **get a free eBook** - Sanctuary.

Details can be found at the end of this book.

Glossary and Historical Information

General terms
Burh: town or village.
Churl: a freeman of the lowest rank, a peasant.
Catamite/Sodomite: homosexual.
Ealdorman: nobility; this became the modern-day earl.
Enga-lond: the Anglo-Saxon name for England.
Englisc: the Anglo-Saxon word for English.
Thane: a warrior; what was to become a knight in later centuries.
Thrall: a slave. People might be forced into slavery when they fell upon hard times. Then they could offer their labour to someone wealthy or powerful in exchange for their freedom. This was usually described as putting your head into somebody else's hands.

Book production
Codex: a hand-written book.
Copyist/scribe: person who does the lettering in a codex; they copy texts from existing works.
Gathering: four sheets of vellum sewn together down the middle to form a booklet of 8 pages.
Illuminator/illustrator: the person who creates the major designs and images in a codex.
Rubricator/miniator: the person who adds rubrics, ornate initials and other decorative flourishes to the pages. It was very rare for the scribe, rubricator and miniator to be the

same monk.

Parchment: a kind of durable paper made from the skins of animals, usually pigs, sheep or goats.

Pattern book: a book filled with designs that an artist can use as references.

Pumice stone: a lightweight, coarse black stone that was used to scour ink off pages, much like we would use an eraser today.

Vellum: a high-quality parchment usually made from calf skin.

Religious life

Abbey: a much larger establishment made up of several cloistered buildings and additional structures beyond the cloisters.

Divine offices: the seven periods throughout the day when the monks stop to pray.

Habit: the clothes a monk wears, these consist of, a tunic (plain single piece robe), scapular a garment that hangs from the shoulders but has no arms, and a cowl/ hood, which is a long single piece garment with a hood and wide sleeves. It fitted over the top of the tunic and scapular.

Monastery: a single cloistered religious institution

Refectory: large dining hall where the monks ate their one daily meal

Scriptorium: room used for codex production

Roles in religious institutions

Abbot: leader of the monastery or abbey.

Armarius: the director of the scriptorium; the armarius gave necessary instructions, assigned tasks, distributed writing materials and managed all writing, artwork and collating.

Chamberlain: looked after the money, clothing and accounts. He also had the responsibility of the archives or records.

Cellarer: in charge of the abbey's food supplies and making sure guests were well fed.

Infirmarius: looked after the sick monks and any poor people who needed medical attention.

Librarian: had charge of the copying room and whatever books the abbey owned.

Master of the Novices: looked after the young boys training to become monks.

Porter: guarded the gate and made sure that no-one entered who did not have a right to be admitted.

The Divine Office also known as the Liturgy of the Hours

Nocturnes/ Lauds: 2 or 3am.

Prime: the first hour of the day, at sunrise, 6am.

Terce: the third hour of the day, 9am.

Sext: originally the sixth hour of the day, noon.

Nones: the ninth hour of the day, 3 pm.

Vespers: early evening, also called Evensong, around 6pm.

Compline: last of the seven canonical hours of the Divine Office, around 7pm, after which everyone went to bed.

List of Characters

Brother Galen of Yarmwick: a scribe/ copyist from Thorpe Parva

Brother Alcuin, son of Maccus: an illustrator from the Wold and the Monastery of Thurby in the Wold

Ealdorman Maccus: Alcuin's father

Brother Benesing: the chief of the infirmary, Galen's uncle

Abbot Dyrewine: the head of the whole religious establishment, in this case the Abbey of Yarmwick

Brother Ranig:the armarius

Brother Waerelm: a scribe/ copyist

Brother Offa: an illuminator

Brother Anfred: the librarian

Brother Haenric: a scribe/ copyist

Brother Kenric: the porter, meets everyone at the door

Brother Sledda: the Master of the Boys/ Novices

Brother Haward: the chamberlain

Brother Wiglaf: an assistant in the infirmary

Brother Thored: the cellarer

Brother Tostig: a fat monk

Brother Edlyn: the book binder

Ealdorman Hugh: a local noble, Galen's father

Septimus the Red: a thane and Hugh's right-hand man

Background to the book

This book starts in February 996 AD. It is set in Anglo-Saxon England. The abbey and the villages I mention are my own invention and never existed. I placed the abbey more or less in the Fenland area of England, which is nearish the east coast. However, England at that time was very different, and much marshier. It has been extensively drained since then, so at the time in which the book is set, the Fens were far more extensive than they are today. In my imagination, the Abbey of Yarmwick is on the westernmost edge of the Fens.

I have tried to be historically accurate, but looking back that far is difficult and can always only be a guess. The clothes, food, medicines and ranks, and daily and religious life, are as close as history permits.

At the time, the British Isles was a feudal society subdivided amongst a number of warring kings. In addition, Danes were alternately trading, attempting to settle and raiding all along the coast. Vikings were essentially pirates. If the people were trading peacefully, they were called Danes, if they were raiding, they were called Vikings, but they were often the same people.

England, at the time, was Catholic, and religion pervaded everyday life. Monasteries, abbeys and convents dotted the land. They were centres of learning, and where the majority of books were produced. Monks frequently travelled between various institutions and they also traded and swapped books. There are letters existing today that show that the religious houses borrowed each other's books so that they could make copies. It was the only way the knowledge in those books could be shared.

The two main characters, Galen and Alcuin, are both young. Galen is fifteen and has been working as a scribe for two years already. The view of children has changed markedly over the centuries. The Anglo-Saxons considered you an adult when you turned thirteen. Even before that, most young people were expected to dress and work alongside their elders and behave in the same way as all of them. So, although to us a fifteen-year-old seems very young, in his time Galen would already be considered an adult. In addition, the average life expectancy of a man at that time was just short of thirty-two years. At the age of fifteen, Galen was nearly halfway through his life.

Trigger Warning

When I wrote this book I needed something really bad to happen to the main character, Galen, that would cause him to be injured and ostracised. One of the main themes of this story is about loneliness and not belonging inside a close knit community. The only crime I could think of that could cause such a situation was rape. Unfortunately, to this day, rape victims are often blamed for what happened to them, they were asking for it, is a common accusation. They are frequently marginalised and cut off from their family and friends and people may make assumptions about the victim and how they can act towards them. Because Galen is a man, he might also be suspected of being a homosexual because he was raped by another man, that whole, he was asking for it, situation again.

I was focussed on Galen's misfortune. But I did land up with the two antagonist of this story as homosexuals. It is not my intention to portray homosexuals as bad or evil people, they aren't. I was merely trying to reflect the beliefs and consequences of the time which comes out in the conversations of the various characters. The views represented in the book are not my views but they may be upsetting to people in the modern era.

Chapter 1

The last character he wrote wasn't as clear as he would have liked, so Galen cleaned it by gently scraping the ink away with his knife. Then he pointed the pen nib toward himself and, with three deft cuts, sharpened it and squared off the tip to ensure crisp lettering. Then he cut into the tip for a fine flow of ink. The whole process took seconds, during which he glanced at his fellow scribes and illuminators. There were four rows of them, all with their heads bowed and their black hoods pulled up to keep themselves warm.

The pen was getting short, and he wondered whether it was worth starting on a new one or just continuing with the current one. He looked down at the wicker basket on the floor on his right-hand side. It was nearly full of the stubby remains of pens he'd already used up and discarded today.

As it was late afternoon and nearly time for Nones, he decided he'd keep going with what he had. He dipped his pen into the inkhorn. His black ink was running low. There was a second inkhorn set into a hole in the desk above the first that held his red ink. He'd not used as much red today as he usually did.

Then again, he'd spent much of his day happily marking out the spaces for the illuminated capitals and the illustrations for the book of hours for his current project. It meant there was less copying than usual, and also less need for the red ink.

Despite the disgraceful nature of his arrival at the Abbey of Yarmwick, Galen thanked God each day that they had allowed him in. As the youngest child with eight surviving older siblings, it would always be his fate to become a monk. Since he had been born small and remained small, it was the only occupation he could usefully do in this age that honoured warriors above all else.

"The runt", Wilnoth, his oldest brother, had called him. He was twelve years Galen's senior and was already a mighty thane in his father's company when Galen was just a boy. He'd spoken without heat, merely stating a fact. Fulk, the second eldest, on the other hand, had taken great glee from singling Galen out with the name.

Aside from his small stature, Galen had a slim frame, fine features and was fairer than his brothers. He spent more time indoors studying than outdoors playing games, wrestling, and hunting, so his face wasn't browned by the sun and roughened by the wind. Because of this, Fulk added to his taunts that Galen looked like a girl.

Galen's shy nature meant he became tongue-tied in a group and had to work hard not to back away when confronted. So when Fulk made fun of him he could only stand silent, his head bowed in shame, turn beet red, and pray that Fulk, his other brothers and gang of friends, would tire of this sport and wander off.

Back then, when he was still very young, he'd run to his mother to pour his hurts out to her sympathetic ears. When he got older, he would slip unseen back to the hall and his books. So, despite the heavy judgement he got from the brothers of Yarmwick, it was a relief to be in this place of learning. It would always be more comfortable than his father's great hall.

Galen's hand trembled and he lifted it quickly so as not to smudge the page as a wave of pain washed over him. It started in his gut, as it always did, and worked its way down to his nether regions. Galen gripped his penknife more tightly, driving his nails into his palm to distract from the pain. It was getting worse, which wasn't unusual towards the end of the day. There wasn't a thing he could do about it. He curled forward, his shoulders arching round in an exaggerated stoop. When he wasn't writing he'd wrap both arms about himself. It took iron discipline not to do it when he was at his work.

Most of Galen's day was spent perched at his desk, copying out manuscripts. The only time he left the scriptorium was when he went to church for the Divine Office, the refectory for the daily meal and the dormitory for bed. The lack of movement was a relief. It was the only thing that helped when the pain got bad. It was just as well he had an aptitude to be a scribe, or they might have set him to harder physical work in the abbey gardens or the kitchens.

Instead, he had a steeply sloped desk upon which he rested the gathering of eight pages of vellum he was writing on.

Above him extended a second book holder with a similar short shelf upon which sat the codex he was copying from. To his left was a large window. It provided an excellent source of light, but in midwinter a flow of cold air washed down the glass onto him, chilling his hands and his left shoulder. Galen blew his fingertips to warm them and watched the mist of his breath flurry away.

He reached up to the source work and the stretch caused another twinge of pain. He pulled at a flat, triangular, lead weight that was resting on the pages, keeping them open. The weight was attached to a string and a similar triangle hung over the back of the desk as a counterbalance. He had an identical weight on the manuscript he was working on. Aside from that, he held his penknife in his left hand, resting horizontally across the page, also keeping the pages flat, while he held his pen in the other hand, at right angles to the vellum as he wrote.

Galen reached the end of his eight-page gathering of vellum. At the bottom of the sheet, in the white space below the text, he wrote the catchword vertically along the outer edge of the page. It was the first word of the next section of text he'd work on when he started on the next gathering of eight pages. The catchword would help him find where he needed to start. Brother Edlyn would also use it to work out which gathering went with which, when he came to binding all the gatherings together into a book.

It gave him a sense of satisfaction when he finished a page and could lean back and admire the neat, even lines of black and red text marching across the parchment. If Brother Anfred, the librarian, allowed it, he could examine the complete work after it had been through everyone's hands. The illuminated lettering and the little artworks gleaming in the light completed and made perfect the work he had contributed to.

Galen placed the completed gathering in the slot under his desk and looked around for Brother Ranig, the armarius. He provided the brothers with all their scribing needs, from ink and vellum, to goose feathers for pens. He also allocated the works to be copied to the various scribes, and he would decide which illustrator would paint the images and capitals in the blanks Galen had left for them.

Galen's breath caught as he saw that Brother Ranig was nearly at the back of the room where he'd placed Galen on his first day in the scriptorium. Fortunately, his work was good enough to earn him a window seat, but that was the only concession he got.

A black scowl marred Brother Ranig's face. It was always the same with the armarius. He was the brother who'd taken most violently against Galen. He'd been open in his calls to have Galen expelled from the abbey. In fact, he'd made it plain that he thought they should put Galen to death.

'For didn't his own father disown him?' Ranig had said in the chapter house.

It still pained Galen when he remembered that excruciating meeting, focused on him and his fate.

Because of his enmity, Brother Ranig only spoke to Galen when strictly necessary. So now he glared at Galen from below darkly lowered brows. He was a tall man in his thirties, with craggy features and permanent, dark stubble on his chin and his tonsure. It was as if his body reflected his prickly nature. Galen might even have found that thought amusing if he wasn't so afraid of Ranig.

Now he stared at the man, trying to guess what he wanted, but came up blank and started to panic.

'Idiot!' Ranig muttered, thrusting his hand towards the slot under Galen's desk, coming so close that Galen smelled his sour sweat and had to sit back to avoid being bumped.

It caused pain, but he didn't dare show that to Ranig, it would only please the man. The armarius pulled out the completed gathering and stomped away before Galen could ask him for a refill of ink. Galen sighed, shaken by the encounter, and gazed down at the glossy virgin vellum, already marked with lines.

Light flickered across the page, first bright, then dark, then bright again. Galen didn't have to look out of the scriptorium window to know that clouds were chasing restlessly across the sky. The weather was as changeable as expected in February. They'd soon need to light their candles to carry on working as dusk approached.

Galen took a shallow, shaky breath and clenched his left hand more tightly around his penknife. The pain in his guts was getting worse. His right hand, barely trembling, moved to his inkhorn, dipped, came back to the page, and traced the characters neatly onto the virgin vellum.

Anyone who saw him wouldn't know, from the movement of his writing, what agony he was living through. He couldn't bear it if they worked it out.

The fingertips of his left hand felt sticky. He forced his hand open slowly and stared blankly at the wounds he'd inflicted with his nails. Bruised and broken skin beaded with blood.

Galen put his penknife on the desk ledge and placed his pen in the small hole above the ink pots, beside his red ink pen. Then he searched with his fingertips under his desk for his black kerchief. He pressed the kerchief against his fresh injuries and squeezed his hand closed about it. The cloth felt hard; the creases set with dried blood. He'd have to wash it again soon.

He looked up to see whether anyone had noticed what he was doing. They hadn't. They seldom did. Today they were even less likely to.

Despite the silence, there was a palpable excitement in the scriptorium. It had gone on for several days now. They were anticipating the arrival of a new brother.

Their lives were so circumscribed in the abbey that anything new was enthusiastically anticipated. But this man was even more special because he was a great illuminator. He would be an honoured member of the brotherhood. So happy were the monks to welcome Alcuin, that last night Brother Haward, the chamberlain, had moved Galen to the least-favoured, draughty bed by the door because they wanted his old bed for their new arrival.

Galen had not demurred. There would be no point. But it left him feeling bitter towards the man who'd ousted him. It probably made him the only person in the room with no wish to meet the famous Brother Alcuin.

No, that wasn't entirely true. He was curious about the new man. He'd found, during his two years at the abbey, that he liked manuscripts. He had no talent as an illustrator. He was merely a copyist. But he liked the pictures, the illuminated capitals and the marginalia that brought his writing to colourful life.

So a traitorous part of him wanted to see the works of Alcuin of Maccus. Surely they had to be extraordinary to cause such excitement amongst his fellow scribes.

In fact, they had discussed in their chapter house meetings how they could lure this talented illustrator away from his monastery at Thurby. The abbot, in the end, had declared that the honour of working at Yarmwick would surely be a sufficient draw. He was proven correct.

A couple of weeks after the abbot had sent his invitation, he'd read a letter to the assembled monks informing them that Brother Alcuin was on his way. Ever since that day, the sense of anticipation had been building in the abbey. During the periods of the day when speech was permitted, the brothers would calculate and recalculate how many days it might take Brother Alcuin to make the journey from his monastery to Yarmwick.

Galen couldn't stop himself from making similar calculations of his own, even though he had reason to be wary of the new arrival. It wasn't just the black stain on his own reputation; Ealdorman Maccus, Alcuin's father, had declared a blood feud against Galen's family. It was widely believed that Galen's grandfather had murdered one of the women of the house of Maccus, although he had denied doing so till the day of his death.

Perhaps, in this one instance, it was a good thing that Galen's father had disowned him. It might keep him safe from any attempt Brother Alcuin might make to avenge his family name.

Chapter 2

Alcuin took his time getting to the Abbey of Yarmwick. He was excited about the prospect of joining this prestigious institution, but to be safe on the road he'd joined a group of merchants heading south. Some were going all the way to Lundenburh; most were going shorter distances to local markets. Either way, travelling in a group was the best way to protect lives and property from attack by brigands.

The added advantage for Alcuin was the wide diversity of people he met and the tales they told. All of which stimulated his imagination and would inspire his illustrations. Aside from that, he enjoyed taking in the scenery as it gradually changed from the gently rolling hills of the Wold, dotted about with sheep, to the flatness of the Fens where farmland was gradually being wrested from the marshes, and the churls in their fields stopped tending to their rows of crops and watched the travellers pass by.

As afternoon approached, Alcuin left the safety of his fellow travellers to peel off to his final destination. He walked the last few miles alone, past the small village of Yarmwick and down a narrow, raised lane that threaded its way through the marshes and on to the abbey. The sky seemed vast on this open plain, and great sheets of clouds streaked across it. The bitingly cold wind blew straight off the sea and was so strong that Alcuin had to lean forward to make progress. He wondered whether being on the marshes was the healthiest place to live. At this time of year there were precious few insects, but he imagined that, come summer, the place would be buzzing with all manner of winged beasts.

Perhaps it wouldn't be so bad, as they had drained the land around the abbey to create the flat, open fields upon which they grew the food to support the community, he thought as he passed by them. An orchard filled with leafless, dripping trees occupied the field to the left of the road, edged by a substantial ditch. They also used the ditch-work as a defensive structure that encircled the abbey.

And now, after a week of walking, Alcuin stood before the abbey gates. There, despite the sharp wind, he stopped to take a proper look at what was to be his new home. He liked what he saw. The abbey was made up of a substantial collection of buildings, the largest of which was the church. He'd been watching the spire of the church grow larger and taller for some time as he'd made his way towards it. Yarmwick was richer and more famous than the monastery he'd grown up in and most of the buildings here, including the church, were built from wood.

Alcuin took a deep breath to control his excitement and building anticipation as he reached for the bell at the abbey foregate and gave it a good, solid couple of tugs. No sooner had the bell ceased its clanking than a thin, bent-over old monk shot out of the porter's lodge, hurried through the cemetery and craned his neck up to examine the new arrival. He beamed at Alcuin, revealing a mouth where only three teeth still clung on.

'Bless me and bless the Lord, for you must surely be Brother Alcuin,' the old monk said as he pushed open the gate. 'Come in, come in! I am Brother Kenric, the porter. So you have finally arrived. We have been in daily expectation of seeing you.'

'Thank you for your kind welcome, Brother Kenric,' Alcuin said, and held firmly onto his bag of belongings, for the old man was trying to take it off him. Thankfully, he didn't insist. Alcuin couldn't have allowed such an old man to carry his goods when he himself was young, fit and healthy.

'Come, I'll take you to the abbot first. He wants to show you around personally,' Brother Kenric said.

He bowed to Alcuin several times, even though they were brothers of the same order and equal in God's eyes, and hurried off, skipping every so often in his haste.

The entrance to the abbey was via the church. Alcuin looked around with interest as they passed through the lobby of the church and across the narthex, a corridor along the narrow end of the church that led to a door on the opposite side. It didn't give Alcuin much chance to take in the interior of the church. It smelled strongly of timber and incense, and was more highly ornamented than he'd expected. But the darkness of the late afternoon made it difficult to make out more than that.

'This way,' Brother Kendrick said, holding a door open. He

looked impatient as he waited for Alcuin, and then scurried on into a cloister. Here the air was still, and warmer, and the central quadrangle was a green square of short, mown grass.

'That's the scriptorium,' Brother Kenric said of the door on the left as they walked down one covered corridor. 'The abbot will show you that himself. The refectory is before us, the kitchen across the green on the right, the dormitory is above the scriptorium. We are very neatly organised.'

Then they were through the cloisters and out into the wind again, and an area with a scattering of other buildings.

'The guest house,' Brother Kenric said of a long, low, wooden building that looked like a great hall that stretched out towards them. 'Behind that are the abbey pools where we farm our fish, the herb garden and the infirmarius's house. A big, strong man like you won't be needing him though.'

They veered left along the path, through the pea fields where only a few hardy crops still hung on, and up to a smart, modern, stone building. Alcuin had been told by the abbot of his old monastery that Abbot Dyrewine of Yarmwick was the youngest son of a powerful family with connections to the king. He was known as a canny political operator, so his appearance came as a surprise to Alcuin. He was a very plain, comfortable-looking man. He was bald with a round, pale face and rosy cheeks which made his bushy, caterpillar-like eyebrows stand out. He looked like a man who never raised his voice, and his eyes twinkled as he shook Alcuin's hand in welcome, enveloping it with both his hands.

'No doubt you're tired from your journey and would like nothing better than to get clean, have some food and put your feet up,' Abbot Dyrewine said. 'But I'm afraid the brothers who work in the scriptorium would never forgive me if I didn't take you to meet them immediately. They have been in daily expectation of your arrival.'

'I am similarly eager to meet them,' Alcuin said, touched by his welcome. 'The fame of your abbey is such that I am honoured to be invited to work here.'

'Very prettily said,' Abbot Dyrewine said with an approving nod. 'Now come, I'll introduce you.'

Chapter 3

The scriptorium door swung open and Galen, along with every other bowed head, looked up in anticipation. Abbot Dyrewine stood on the threshold. The abbot was the least intimidating man Galen had ever laid eyes on. He was scruffy, of average height and tending towards pudginess.

He had only spoken to Galen once, shortly after he'd arrived, when he'd welcomed him to the brotherhood. He'd shown through neither words nor expression what he thought of Galen. At the time, it had been a comfort.

The abbot beamed at the assembly as he announced, 'Brothers, I bring you Brother Alcuin. He has finally arrived, bearing a gift of one of his codices from his monastery. He has also brought two of his pattern books. The illuminators amongst you will be eager to use them as a guide and for inspiration. Come and make him welcome.'

Here, then, was another sign of this illuminator's standing. The abbot rarely made a show of introducing new brothers. Yet here he was, accompanying this young monk who looked about eagerly.

No shyness from him, Galen thought. Why should he hang back or make any attempt at modesty? He was a fine-looking man, taller than the abbot, with broad shoulders. He wouldn't look out of place as a thane. He was handsome too, with intelligent, clear blue eyes and regular features set in his face, in perfect symmetry. What remained of his hair, below the tonsure, was thick, golden curls.

The brothers slipped down from their benches and surged around this handsome arrival. They were all talking at once, trying to attract his attention and welcoming him. Several made for the codices he laid on the librarian's desk at the front of the scriptorium.

'How beautiful!' Brother Haenric, one of the copyists, said, as he opened the codex.

'Let me see,' Brother Offa said, pushing to the front of the crowd and snatching up one of the pattern books. 'We illustrators should be given the first look.'

Galen couldn't stay where he was, the only man who hadn't moved from his desk. It would occasion comment. He slowly eased himself down from the high chair, being careful not to jar his body, and took a few steps towards the huddle of excited monks. This was far enough. He wouldn't stand out here, and he was unlikely to be jostled.

'Look at these colours,' Brother Offa gasped, as he lifted the book high for the men clustered around him to see.

Galen strained to look, but he was short and couldn't see over the crowd.

'You truly are blessed with a rare talent,' Brother Offa said.

There was a murmur of agreement and a gasp of surprise

from the gathered men as Offa revealed each new image.

Galen wished he had the courage, and the physical strength, to push himself to the front of the crowd so he could see this wonder. But he had neither. His face twitched unhappily as he lowered his head and considered everybody's feet. They were all wearing brown leather day shoes. Their robes were supposed to be short enough for the ankles to show, as was the Rule of St Benedict, but in winter many of them had pulled their breeches down to meet the shoes and then wrapped strips of cloth around the shoes and ankles to keep their feet warm. Hours of sitting nearly motionless at a high table resulted in icy cold toes.

Most of the monks also wore woollen, fingerless gloves to prevent their fingers from growing numb and clumsy from the cold. The gloves were knitted at home and delivered to the brothers by visiting family. Since Galen no longer had a family, he didn't have gloves either. In the depths of the winter he would wrap the same strips of cloth he had on his feet, around his hands, but it was a cumbersome solution. For that reason, he did it less than he might have otherwise.

'You've all had a good look now,' Abbot Dyrewine said, 'and you will have further opportunity to see Brother Alcuin's work when he produces his first codex for us. Now, I will continue showing Brother Alcuin around our abbey. As it is nearly time for Nones, you are all welcome to join us for the rest of the tour.'

This suggestion met with universal approval and a rowdy group of monks made their way out of the scriptorium, each competing with the other to get Brother Alcuin's attention. Galen made no move to follow them. He would only end up trailing, unnoticed, behind the crowd.

He watched everyone leave and looked slowly round the room, feeling more alone than he had in a long time. The armarius had also remained and was slowly leafing through Alcuin's codex.

'Brother Ranig?' Galen said, scared to draw this man's attention, but driven by a desire to catch just a glimpse of Alcuin's work. The armarius didn't look up, absorbed by the codex. Galen took a cautious breath and said more loudly, 'Brother Ranig, may... may I see the codex... please?'

Brother Ranig looked up, and he glared for a moment at the speaker, taking in who'd broken into his thoughts.

'No!'

Ranig closed the codex with a snap, tucked it and the two pattern books under his arm, and took them to the locked wooden trunk of codices on the south side of the dais. He pulled a heavy key from his pocket, unlocked the trunk, reverentially placed the books on the top of a pile of codices to be copied, slammed the lid down firmly and locked the padlock. He turned and gave Galen a challenging, pugnacious look.

'What are you waiting for? It will be Nones soon. Go to the church.'

Galen felt crushed. Ranig's denial, and his obvious contempt, felt like an impossible weight pressed onto his shoulders. Ranig charged down the steps of his dais, grabbed Galen by the arm and pushed him out of the scriptorium into the cloister. Then he turned, locked the door and hurried off.

Galen staggered forward and grabbed onto a pillar. He hung on while white dots jumped in his vision. He fought against the pain, clenching his fists tight, and pushed down the tears. Ranig had wrenched at him. He'd pushed him too fast, so that his guts were in flames and his hip bones and spine felt like they'd been filled with boiling lead.

Alcuin was a modest young man, and his welcome was gratifying. He hadn't expected to be greeted as an honoured guest or to be surrounded by excited monks, all pressing his hand in welcome and talking animatedly about his work. He'd have to be careful not to let it make him prideful.

He'd always enjoyed making his illustrations. He'd felt that his work was better than the other manuscripts he'd seen at his old monastery. But he hadn't realised how much better.

He'd been astonished when his old abbot called him to his office and informed him that Dyrewine of the Abbey of Yarmwick had invited Alcuin to join them. The library of Yarmwick was renowned. The king used them for all his official documents, as well as for the production of key manuscripts. To be surrounded by the finest books in the land and to join the greatest thinkers, illuminators, translators and scribes was such a great honour that he was still thrilled by it.

Alcuin had also liked the scriptorium. They'd glazed the astonishing, massive, circular window at the front of the room with clear glass. They'd done the same to the row of windows down the south wall. It was an unaccustomed luxury for Alcuin, who was used to a smaller, darker space in which to work. High above them, great wooden beams supported a wooden shingle roof and the wooden walls and pillars were carved into interwoven, patterned ribbons through which pranced deer, lions, hares and wild boar. He'd never seen anything so ornate before. He was sure it would provide inspiration for his work.

It was the perfect room to work in with its large, widely-spaced desks. The largest and tallest desks were near the window to maximise light for the illuminators and copyists. The narrower desks were against the north wall for the translators, for whom light wasn't as critical.

Now Alcuin was walking through the cloister again, making towards the church, surrounded by an excited group of monks, all introducing themselves at once. Alcuin feared he'd never remember who was who. That was alright, he'd get to know their names soon enough.

'It's a lot to take in, isn't it?' the abbot said with a benevolent smile, as he strolled beside Alcuin.

'It is. Aside from my move from home to the monastery, I've never been anywhere else. This abbey is considerably bigger.'

'Do you like it?' Abbot Dyrewine asked, as he paused to wash his hands at a stone trough, and then stepped into the church.

Alcuin hurried through washing his hands and said, 'It's wonderful.'

Now he could take his time examining this holy structure. Candles had been lit that cast a warm glow and picked everything out in flickering relief.

'I've never been inside such a beautiful church before. It seems that everything that can be carved or painted has been. Even the edges of the benches and the tops of the supporting posts are ornamented and painted.'

'All for the glory of God.'

'It is a magnificent gesture,' Alcuin said, his head flung back so he could get a better view of the painted ceiling of the church.

'I'm glad it meets with your approval. I also hope that it will provide inspiration for the works that you will create for us.'

'I have no doubt about that,' Alcuin said, as they made their leisurely way down the nave. To his right was a side chapel dedicated to St Cuthbert, to his left was a Lady Chapel dedicated to the Virgin Mary. The most magnificent sky blue altar cloth, embroidered with silver thread, adorned the altar in the Lady Chapel. The vividness of the blue struck Alcuin, and he longed to take a closer look, but felt he couldn't pull away from the abbot and following monks now.

'Just in time,' murmured the abbot as he arrived at the choir.

Alcuin realised it was time for Nones and the entire community had started to arrive, including the novices being herded by a monster of a man who appeared to be the Master of the Novices.

The abbey was large indeed. Alcuin tried counting the arriving monks, but got constantly distracted as they introduced him to yet more men. He guessed there were over a hundred men and boys. It was a considerable increase over the twenty that had made up the community of his old monastery home of Thurby.

Chapter 4

The church bell shook Galen into wakefulness just as he'd fallen asleep again. He always found it so difficult to drop off after Nocturns. He inevitably did so only moments before the bell rang to get everyone up again for Prime.

He smothered a sigh and, his eyes still closed, reached for his cowl, which was folded next to his pillow. Thankfully, as it felt like another frosty morning, it was a requirement that you pulled your cowl on while still under the blankets. Galen also thanked God that his cowl was lined with sheepskin. Abbot Dyrewine was a practical man, and Galen had once overheard him saying that he didn't see why his monks should freeze.

Once the cowl was on and the hood pulled over his head, Galen got up and reached for his day shoes, tucked underneath the bed. He much preferred the sheepskin-lined night shoes, but they weren't allowed for the day. After the shoes, he pulled on his gown, the long sleeves of which fell to the tips of his fingers. He took hold of the edge of the sleeves and made fists with his hands, closing them inside the wrapping of the sleeves and blocking the entry of cold air.

All around him, his fellow monks were doing the same. The rule of the abbey allowed no talk at this hour of the morning, so it was eerily silent as nearly a hundred men got dressed. Their monastic rule also required that they raise their hoods. The room was, therefore, soon full of anonymous, black-hooded figures.

The moment they were all dressed, something that only took a couple of minutes, there was a silent rush to the privies. These were in a separate building next door to the dormitory. This required the monks to go downstairs into the cloister, take a right, and then go upstairs again to the privies that had been built to open out onto the river that flowed by the side of the abbey.

Galen never rushed anywhere. It hurt too much to do so, especially this morning. He accepted that he'd get to the privy last and would have to wait till everyone else was done.

So he stood in line and watched the men who'd finished their ablutions heading back down the stairs to the cloister. Although they had their hoods pulled low, Galen occupied his time by identifying each retreating monk.

A man might think that in their black robes they all looked alike, but even without a face or a voice to identify them with, it was still easy to tell one from the other. Brother Haenric walked with a slight lopsided gait as one of his legs was shrivelled by an illness contracted as a child. Brother Waerelm had a peculiar sway to his hips that added to an already effeminate way of speaking. Brother Edlyn always looked like he was marching, as he raised his knees higher than most.

Brother Alcuin emerged from the privy that Galen was standing in front of and brushed past. Galen was certain he hadn't been noticed. He looked back, watching Alcuin trot down the stairs. Even his walk was full of confidence.

Still, it was getting late, and he couldn't hang about. Galen hurried into the privy to do his ablutions. Then he walked to the church as quickly as possible without hurting himself. He wasn't successful. Every step jarred his body and shot an arrow of pain through his viscera.

He took a shaky breath and tried not to cry. It wouldn't help, he knew that well enough. It robbed his mind of the ability to think and left him in a daze through which it was difficult to concentrate.

He was late for Prime too, so he slipped into the church, angling his body so he didn't push the half-open door any wider. The chanting had already started. He shuffled up behind the novices, earning himself a black look from their master, Brother Sledda.

Then he pulled his hood further down and listened for a moment, trying to work out where the singers had got to. In a flat and tuneless voice, he began to sing along. He dropped his head, taking blessed relief in allowing the hood to fall forward all the way, obscuring his face, and lost himself in the power of this communal prayer. As he sang, he sent his own thoughts up to God and begged Him, as he did every day, to bring his suffering to an end.

'Go in peace,' the abbot said at the end of the service.

Since it was still a silent period, the monks merely bowed and filed away to take up their morning chores. For Galen, this meant making his way to the scriptorium. Brother Ranig had brought in several basket-loads of goose feathers. They were already partly prepared for use as they had been dried and hardened in a shed out by the pea field for several months.

Galen planned, therefore, as he did every morning, to strip the quills of their feathers and cut the tip away into a point, ready to be used. As it was winter, he only had about an hour to work on the pens before it would be time for the morning mass of Terce, followed by the chapter meeting.

Several of the other scribes sat in a circle at the front of the scriptorium, some on the dais steps that led to Brother Ranig's desk and what would soon be Brother Alcuin's desk, while the rest sat sideways at their desks, the baskets on the floor in front of them. Galen sat to one side. They never included him in the little group of scribes. At least during the silent periods he didn't feel as left out. During periods when conversation was allowed, he felt the exclusion more powerfully because nobody ever spoke to him.

The situation made him think about Saint Óengus whom they had learned about yesterday in the chapter house. He was a wise man who wished to leave the distractions of daily life and live as a hermit. At first, he'd lived only a mile from the nearest town. But this was reached too easily, and people kept coming to visit him for blessings and insights. So he'd moved further out into the wilderness. Still the people had found him, and so, finally, in desperation, he'd joined a monastery under an assumed name. All to get away from people.

Galen suppressed a sigh as he considered the saint. He'd wanted to be alone and hadn't managed it. Galen, on the other hand, was sociable. Shy as he was, he loved the company of friends and family. He liked nothing better than to hear of each person's little triumphs and to cheer with them when things went well. True, Saint Óengus had communed with angels when he was in his wilderness, but Galen felt it wasn't the same. And here he was, surrounded by men and yet all alone.

He pushed that melancholy thought away and looked across at the illustrators, rubricators and miniators who formed another little circle nearer the window, where they were preparing their brushes in readiness for a day of painting. Brother Alcuin was sitting at the head of that group, already integrated.

The bell sounded for Terce, which broke the period of silence.

'Thank goodness,' Brother Anfred, the librarian, said as he stood and stretched. He was a tall, fair-haired man in his twenties and already a scholar of some renown. Because of this, he was the true leader of the scriptorium, despite Brother Ranig's superior position and age.

Galen liked to hear Brother Anfred's opinions. He had much to say on theology, the lives of the saints and the doctrine of the church. It was precisely this sort of man he'd hoped to meet when he left his father's burh and joined the abbey. Sadly, it hadn't worked out quite the way he had envisaged it.

'Come on,' Anfred said, and the rest of the brothers were quick to follow him as he strolled out towards the church for morning mass.

'What do you think will be on the agenda for today's

chapter meeting?' Brother Waerelm said, as he hurried after the librarian.

Galen shuddered as he watched that monk leave, followed by the rest. While Ranig was brusque and violently physical, Waerelm was another open enemy, but he was more subtly undermining. As Galen followed the brothers out, he saw Waerelm lean close to Brother Offa and whisper something into his ear. He also took every opportunity to drip poison with every piece of gossip he shared. It wasn't only about Galen either. Waerelm took pleasure in undermining everyone. He would curry favour with one brother by carrying tales about another.

Galen tried to banish his fears about Waerelm during the brief service of Terce, but wasn't entirely successful. He was still mulling over why some people chose to be destructive of their fellows as he followed the monks on their short walk from the church to the adjoining room of the chapter house.

Galen, as always, arrived last and settled on the lowest step, right by the door. In that way he avoided drawing attention to himself. The room was filled with a great cacophony of voices that bounced and amplified off the walls as the monks chatted to each other. This large octagonal tower of a room was the noisiest in the abbey, which was a consequence of its design.

Galen's uncle, Brother Benesing, the infirmarius, had once told him that in the early days of the abbey, when he'd first arrived, there had been a single bench around the outer wall of the chapter house. But as the number of monks had grown, they'd had to create a stepped structure, much like an amphitheatre. So now the chapter house had three layers of staggered seating. This newer arrangement reduced the effectiveness of the chamber. His uncle had told him that in its original layout, a man on one side of the room could be heard on the other, even if he merely whispered. Galen would have liked to have seen that.

Galen had mixed feelings about the chapter meeting. It was an opportunity to hear what was going on in the abbey. All the reports on trade and abbey announcements were made at the chapter meeting, such as welcoming the new illustrator. That he enjoyed.

What he didn't like was that any misdemeanours were also reported here, and punishments pronounced by the community. When Galen had fallen ill, he'd been unable to work or take part in the Divine Office. Once he'd recovered, he had to prostrate himself on the floor in front of the abbot and beg forgiveness for deviating from the rule.

It was merely a formality. Everyone had to do it at some point in their life at the abbey. But Galen had felt the disapproving stares of the monks upon him as he'd lain there on the cold slabs. It had made him wish he could crawl away into some dark nook and never be seen again.

Once the business of the abbey was complete, the talk would move to theology. They'd either listen to a reading, or one of the senior monks would lead a discussion on the life of a saint.

'Today we will continue considering Saint Óengus,' the abbot said. 'We discussed his early years yesterday, but his later life was equally informative. Once Saint Maelruain, the abbot of his monastery, divined who he was, he welcomed Óengus with open arms. The two men then embarked upon a work of great learning, the Martyrology of Tallaght, a copy of which we have in our library. Isn't that so, Brother Anfred?'

'Quite true, my abbot. It is also on the list of books I believe we should copy, for there is great wisdom in its pages, and a most complete list of the Irish saints and their deeds.'

Galen's ears pricked up at that. Reading brought him solace, distraction and food for thought. A book on saints, therefore, would be fascinating. He always wondered what, exactly, it took to be a saint. A great deal of fortitude appeared to be a universal constant. The saints all seemed to be such bold individuals, and so clear about what they wanted to achieve for the glory of God.

Chapter 5

Alcuin was pleased that he was finally getting to do some proper work. Up till now he'd been engaged in the rites and rituals of the abbey. That was fine. It was the structure of their lives. Alcuin didn't mind it, but he couldn't wait for all of that business to be over with so he could get down to his true love of painting.

To his surprise, the abbot accompanied him back to the scriptorium. That appeared to be an unusual thing to do, if the wide-eyed amazement of the brothers who'd already arrived was anything to go by.

The abbot smiled indulgently at his monks and, spotting the armarius, said, 'Brother Ranig, have you prepared a desk for our new illuminator?'

The armarius bowed low at the question and said, 'I've placed the young man on the dais beside myself, Abbot Dyrewine. It is the best position for light so that his work may not be hampered.'

'Thank you,' Alcuin said, taking in the high desk with its attached chair and footrest so worn that a couple of dimples showed where generations of monks had rested their feet. 'I am grateful, Brother Ranig, but there really isn't any need to give me such an exalted position. I'm sure any seat would be acceptable in this fine scriptorium.'

'Nonsense!' the abbot said. 'Your modesty does you honour, but it isn't necessary. You'll be working very hard for us, you know. I want you to produce many fine masterpieces for Yarmwick. It is especially important as we approach the millennium. You may as well accept the desk we have allocated to you. It will ensure you produce your best work.'

Alcuin bowed rueful acceptance.

The abbot grinned at him, gave his back a couple of powerful, friendly slaps and said, 'Now, let's see what we can do about finding you a scribe. Step into the library with me.'

Alcuin was even more surprised now, but followed the abbot, trailed by Brother Ranig, into a smaller, darker room at the back of the scriptorium. It was filled with shelves. On these they'd stacked a wide variety of books, some leather-bound, others with fine embroidery covers, some with only a wooden cover and more yet that were mere bundles of vellum sewn together without a cover at all.

'The best scribe?' Alcuin said uncertainly.

'Of course! We need a man with a fine, even hand that does justice to your illuminations,' the abbot said as he gave a nod to the librarian, Brother Anfred.

'The thing is,' Alcuin said, 'in my last monastery, I just did my paintings on whichever codex needed it next.'

'That's how we usually do it too,' Abbot Dyrewine said, beaming at him. 'But we want the manuscripts you will produce here in Yarmwick to be the very best. We can't have your illuminations devalued by a cramped or uneven script.'

Alcuin could see that there was no point in arguing, so bowed acceptance and waited. The librarian had been waiting for this moment and brought out five specimen sheets, which he laid in a row along his desk.

'Have a look, my boy. Which man's hand would best honour your illuminations?' Abbot Dyrewine said.

'My abbot, surely in your abbey they are all just as good, one to the other.'

'How can you say that, Alcuin, you whose eye is so acute? Come and look at these scripts. You'll see they are all different. They are each a reflection of their writer's own style. These are our five best scribes and you shall choose one to work with you from now on.'

Alcuin stepped up to the row of sheets and took a closer look. Every scribe produced specimen sheets so that clients could choose a style of text for their documents. For this reason, each sheet had blocks of text in a variety of different fonts.

Alcuin supposed the abbot was right. Not only did each man produce a variety of different fonts, but each one of their handwriting styles was different to the next. Since he'd never had a say before, he'd not bothered his head over it. Perhaps it would be an interesting exercise to make this choice.

The first scribe's work was heavy and dark. Now that he considered it, he thought he'd like something lighter. The next also didn't suit him as it was a little too fine, too delicate, to stand against his ornate illustrations. The next two also didn't find favour - the one seemed a bit too cramped, the other had a strange unevenness that Alcuin didn't like. He liked the last sheet instantly, though. The lettering was flawless. Not a single mistake marred the words that marched in perfect lines so evenly spaced he couldn't believe a rule wasn't used to make them so.

'This one,' Alcuin said, firmly. 'I would like this to be the scribe I work with.'

'Brother Galen,' the armarius said in a hollow voice, his lips twisting as if they had forced him to swallow a mouthful of bile.

The abbot gave him a knowing smile and said, 'It is Alcuin's wish, Ranig.'

'Is there something wrong?' Alcuin said. 'If you don't wish it, I can choose another, but...'

'But what, my son?'

'It seems to me his hand is the fairest of the lot. Now that you gave me the choice, it would be harsh to have it removed.'

'Quite so, and if we didn't want Galen to be selected, we shouldn't have shown you any of his work, should we?'

Alcuin flushed and said, 'Forgive me, my abbot, I didn't mean any disrespect.'

'I am not offended,' the abbot said, amusement dancing in his eyes. 'Ranig! How old is Galen? He must be near Alcuin's age, must he not?'

'I'd say a year or two younger,' Ranig muttered, still rigidly disapproving. 'He arrived shortly after he'd attained his majority and he's about fifteen now.'

'So they'll be able to work together for years to come. It sounds like an ideal partnership.'

'Galen is a sickly youth,' Brother Ranig said in a condemnatory tone.

'But you aren't so unchristian as to wish that his infirmity carries him off anytime soon, are you, Ranig?'

It would have been imprudent to disagree with the abbot, but it surprised Alcuin to see that the armarius had to make a considerable effort before he could say, colourlessly, 'Of course not, my abbot.'

'Good, then it is decided. Give Brother Galen his new directions. I look forward to seeing the completed codex.'

Alcuin burned to ask the armarius more about the mysterious Brother Galen, but one look at his thunderous face as they made their way back to the scriptorium was enough to quell his tongue. Instead, he wracked his brain trying to conjure up the image of Brother Galen. The name was unfamiliar to him. He was certain they hadn't been introduced. He'd paid special attention to all the scribes, and yet he couldn't picture anyone called Galen.

'Go to your desk,' Ranig said, as they stepped into the scriptorium. 'I'll give Galen the script to be copied. The abbot wants you to illustrate the work of the life of St Cuthbert. You'll have to discuss the details of the layout within the codex with Galen. But he will have to look at it first and gain an understanding of the text. While he is doing that and copying out the first gathering of the codex, I'll give you some other work to illuminate. Since you like Galen so much, you may as well work on the book of hours he's nearly completed,' Ranig said with heavy irony. 'Brother Offa has been doing the illustrations and capitals for that, but no doubt he'll be delighted to have your collaboration. Brother Waerelm will have to finish the text for the book of hours. The abbot will not want to wait to see your first completed masterpiece.'

'Yes, Brother,' Alcuin said, trying to be as polite as possible to assuage Ranig's very obvious sense of injustice.

His bitterness was surprising. Alcuin felt like he'd made some fatal blunder in his selection of a scribe. So, as he slipped into his seat, he kept watching Brother Ranig. The armarius picked up the original manuscript and a bundle of gatherings of vellum and stomped to the back of the room. He stopped before a young man at the window. He was just dipping his quill into the inkwell but looked up as Ranig approached. Alcuin couldn't hear what they said, but Galen's eyes flickered briefly to examine Alcuin's face and then back to the armarius.

Galen was a small, very thin young man. He looked paler than any of the other monks, which was an achievement in late winter. He apparently wasn't getting enough sleep, judging by the black rings under his eyes. His nose had been broken and healed again, slightly out of kilter, but he had a pleasant face for all that, with fine features and a smattering of pale freckles.

He listened closely to the armarius, his face reflecting deepening surprise. Then he nodded acceptance as Brother Ranig handed over the book about St Cuthbert and took away the book Galen had been copying from, as well as the half-finished gathering that Galen had been writing on.

Alcuin had expected Galen to look at him again, but he didn't. He opened the new codex and started leafing slowly through it. Alcuin was left to wonder why he'd never noticed Galen before, because even his face hadn't stirred the least memory of him.

He was also waiting. It was usual for the scribe to decide

the layout of a book. They would outline the areas for the images and mark out squares where they wanted illuminated capitals.

The ancient scribe Alcuin had worked the most with in his old monastery had even listed the colours he had to use. Alcuin hoped that Brother Galen wouldn't be as prescriptive. At least he was a younger man and hopefully more easily swayed or cajoled.

Galen's mind reeled at the armarius's order. He was to be the scribe of Brother Alcuin's first codex! Surely there had to be some mistake? Surely they'd come to their senses and take the project away from him.

But for the moment he had the most exciting manuscript he'd had to work on so far. In the two years he'd been at the abbey he'd progressed gradually from copying out dry-as-dust legal documents, to gospels and, finally, once he'd proved himself as a reliable scribe, they had given him a book of hours.

He never expected to be working with the star illustrator for the abbey. And yet, the abbot must have sanctioned this wondrous event himself. For hadn't he disappeared into the library with Brother Alcuin and Brother Ranig? It had to be right then, didn't it? It was an interesting project too: the life of Saint Cuthbert as written by the Venerable Bede.

But if it was a mistake, he didn't have a moment to lose. He had to see and do as much as he could before it was taken away from him. Galen opened the ancient codex Brother Ranig had given him and examined the first few lines. These were words dictated two hundred years ago by a man of such great learning that they had made him a Doctor of the Church. As a boy, Galen had memorised Bede's Ecclesiastical History of the English People. It was the most interesting and best written book he'd ever come across. From that moment on he'd devoured any other of Bede's codices he could lay his hands on.

Up till now, he hadn't come across this hagiography. It looked like it was a fascinating story. Galen couldn't recall a discussion of Saint Cuthbert in the chapter house. All he knew of the saint were the stories he'd heard of him at home. It was always difficult to know from them what was the truth and what was embellishment. Much in the codex was new to him, and far more reliable, which added to his excitement.

'Brother Galen?' a voice said, right beside his ear.

Galen jumped, turned, and found himself face to face with Brother Alcuin. His first foolish thought was that he was even more handsome up close. His second, more panicked worry, was the question of why he was there.

'Yes?' he said breathlessly.

'Forgive me, Brother Galen, I know it's the custom for the scribe to decide on the type, placement and number of images to go into a codex,' Alcuin said, 'but I was hoping we might discuss the project together.'

Galen stared open-mouthed at Alcuin. Not because of the request, prettily made as it was. It was Alcuin's attitude that surprised him. He realised in a flash that Alcuin knew nothing of his reputation. If he did, he wouldn't be so friendly.

'You... you want to discuss the images?'

'I hope you don't mind,' Alcuin said, and placed a chunky book, really just a collection of sewn together gatherings, on the desk. 'This is my pattern book. I thought it might provide some inspiration. I mean, I'm sure you have your own ideas, but illustration is what I'm best at.'

Galen blinked owlishly at Alcuin's smiling face, then looked down at the codex as Alcuin flipped it open to the first page. For one brief, heaven-sent moment Galen was looking at the great Alcuin's illuminations. Now he'd be able to see what was so special about his talent.

Galen stifled a gasp of surprise. Two farmers, their laughing faces gazing up at him from the page, wound their way around a stook of wheat. About them were twined images of crops and harvest. Galen had never seen anything to equal it, and a hurt, almost as deep as that in his guts, took a hold of his heart. How he longed to emulate that perfection or, failing that, just draw nearer to its creator. That neither was possible was almost beyond bearing.

'Did you... is this an image of your own creation?' Galen asked, partly to distract himself and partly because he was curious to know.

'It is,' Alcuin said, beaming with pride. 'It is a variation on the theme of harvest from a book of hours, as you'll be aware. But this one I drew myself. As with most of the illustrations here. Although some are patterns and images I've seen and liked well enough to want to duplicate. Some other pictures in this book are interesting, or things I wouldn't have thought of drawing, and others still are merely useful reminders of how to draw some basics.'

'I see,' Galen said, as he turned the page over with a

trembling hand. He hoped Brother Alcuin didn't notice how he was shaking. Now he was looking at a two-page spread of illuminated letters from A to Z. The level of detail was astonishing, as were the life-like images of birds and butterflies that flitted between the letters or poked out from behind curving, ornamental vines.

'Do you know that we'll be working on a book about the life of Saint Cuthbert?'

'Brother Ranig told me,' Alcuin said. 'It sounds a good deal more interesting than the Psalter that I had as my last project.'

'Do you know anything about his life?'

'Of course, he's one of Enga-lond's best known saints.'

'Yes,' Galen said.

A world of possibilities was opening up before him. This project with Brother Alcuin could change everything. With this codex he could do more than merely copy what had gone before. This thought was so audacious it nearly took his breath away. Brother Alcuin was like a revelation with his suggestion that they might do something different.

'Maybe,' Galen said cautiously, 'you should consider his life. Think about the parts you like best, then we could illustrate that.'

Alcuin grinned happily at him and said, 'What an excellent idea. Once I've thought about that, we can also discuss the capitals and marginalia. Unless you like what's in your original copy, I suggest we come up with our own designs.'

Galen felt irresistibly swept away by Alcuin's enthusiasm. A smile hovered, ready to break out on his lips. But the sudden thought that he had to be careful wiped his happiness out. Brother Alcuin didn't know about him. He doubted he'd want to continue the project with him once he did find out.

'The first chapter is about how a child predicted that Cuthbert would one day become a bishop.'

'Ah yes, that was when Cuthbert was still a boy himself, wasn't it?'

'They were at play together,' Galen said. That was a part of Cuthbert's story that everybody knew.

'It's a good place to start. I'll get planning,' Alcuin said, as he gave a satisfied nod and went back to his desk.

Galen watched him go and took a careful, shuddering breath. He had to force himself to be calm. He might not have the talent for art that Alcuin had, but he could write. He would ensure that none of the beauty Alcuin would produce would be marred by an imperfection in his letters. In the meantime, he prayed that Alcuin would continue in his friendly way and not freeze him out like all the others had. This, he feared, was a futile hope.

Alcuin had a good feeling about Brother Galen after their chat. He'd not only been open to discussing what illustrations might go into the book, he'd also made a good suggestion. What was odd was that he'd looked frightened to be approached. Alcuin couldn't figure out why. He knew he was tall and athletic, but he'd never met somebody he intimidated before.

That was a mystery, and every now and then Alcuin flicked a curious look in Brother Galen's direction to see what he was up to and try to understand what was going on. Galen first worked his way through the book, probably getting a feel for it. Then he placed the codex on the copying shelf, open at the first page. He laid out the first gathering of eight pages on his desk, gave it a good rubdown with a pumice stone, and then applied the chalk.

Then Galen paused for a moment as if gathering his thoughts, took out his black ink pen, dipped it into the inkhorn and began copying. Whenever Alcuin saw the start of a book, he thought of it like the beginning of a long journey. A man needed to gird his loins, gather his courage, and expect that it would take a long time. Many codices took at least a year to produce. A codex as intricate as the one he and Brother Galen were creating would probably take longer.

A bell sounded through the abbey for Sext. A couple of the men working in the scriptorium looked up at the sound, acknowledging the time, then went back to their work. Light was such a scarce resource that anyone involved in manuscript production was exempt from the offices of Sext and None in Yarmwick, just as they had been at Alcuin's old monastery. They would all work through till dinner time.

Alcuin noted that Galen didn't react to the sound of the bell. Now that he'd started writing, he sat as still as a stone. The only motion in his body over the next couple of hours was the rhythm of his right hand dipping into the inkwell and then tracing across the vellum.

Maybe that was why Alcuin hadn't noticed him, he thought. One bowed and tonsured or hooded head looked much like another.

As the abbey bell chimed the hour for dinner, Alcuin slipped from his seat and hurried to the back of the room.

'Brother Galen,' he said.

Galen gave a start as he turned towards him, which froze the smile on Alcuin's lips. It was strange that he was still frightened, although he relaxed a bit as he registered who was speaking to him.

'May I see the manuscript now, brother? I'd like to see how it's starting to shape up.'

Galen's eyes dropped to the desktop as he slowly turned the gathering towards Alcuin with his right hand.

Alcuin's instinct had been right. The letters were in perfect proportion to set off his illustrations. 'I knew it,' he murmured.

Galen glanced briefly at him, then sank back in on himself. Alcuin wondered what to do next. Everyone else was packing up and heading to the refectory, but Galen didn't move. Was he waiting for Alcuin to leave?

As there didn't seem to be anything more to do, Alcuin gave Galen a perfunctory smile and hurried after the band of brothers who'd taken him into their circle. Aside from Brother Anfred, the librarian, these were all scribes and illustrators and therefore young men. There were precious few older monks working in the scriptorium. Their eyes lost the keenness necessary for the production of codices.

'Really, Alcuin, what were you thinking?' Brother Waerelm said as he joined them. 'I mean, Galen!'

'Yes? What about Galen?' Alcuin said, surprised by the murmur of agreement that rose from the rest of the brothers.

'He's a damned sodomite, that's what!'

'What?' Alcuin said, surprised and dismayed by this piece of gossip. 'How can you possibly know that?'

'We all know,' Brother Anfred said. 'He was buggered to within an inch of his life and brought to the abbey near death. He spent months in the infirmary, and when he was well enough they should have sent him away. But his uncle interceded for him and they allowed him to stay and join our numbers instead.'

Alcuin cast a quick look behind them and spotted Galen lagging far behind the others, hopefully out of hearing range. 'Who is his uncle? Who can have that much influence?'

'His uncle is Brother Benesing, the head of our infirmary. He has ever had the abbot's ear.'

'Maybe he could tell the abbot something we don't know which made Galen acceptable to join our ranks,' Alcuin said, as they hurried down the cloister.

'Well, if you will be conciliatory, there's no helping you,' Brother Waerelm said, his voice heavy with dissatisfaction.

Alcuin gave him a placatory smile and cast another look in Galen's direction. They'd increased the gap between them. He didn't know why precisely, but he felt sorry for him.

'Still, one good thing came of your arrival,' Waerelm said. 'They ousted him from the corner.'

'What corner?'

'Your bed,' Waerelm said, his smile broadening. 'When he emerged from the infirmarius's house, they put him in the bed in the corner to keep him as far away from the rest of us as possible. It wasn't popular because the corner beds are the favoured spots. Brother Haward was able to make the case that you should have that favoured position instead, and they gave Galen the bed by the door.'

'His place was ceded to me?' Alcuin said.

'That's right. Such are the wages of talent.'

Alcuin got the overwhelming impression that all the brothers were so supportive of this measure that he couldn't demur. He didn't like it, though. He wouldn't blame Galen if he hated him for all that they'd done to him in the name of honouring the new illustrator.

Thankfully, further discussion was curtailed by their arrival in the refectory where silence was required. As was to be expected of a large abbey, the refectory was bigger than his father's hall. The walls were painted with life-sized images of the apostles. At one end of the hall was a raised dais with a long, bench-like table. The abbot and senior monks occupied that table. Above them was another larger-than-life fresco of the Last Supper.

The rest of the refectory was filled with four rows of tables set at right angles to the abbot's table. These filled rapidly with hungry monks. Dinner was the only meal of the day, and Alcuin's stomach was growling in eager expectation of what they might serve.

The Abbey of Yarmwick was a strict adherent of the rules laid down by St Benedict, so the basis for the meal was always a vegetable pottage, mainly made from cabbage at this time of the year, accompanied by beans, bread and ale. What kept things interesting was the little side plate of supplemental food. As today was Thursday, Alcuin's mouth was salivating in expectation of some fish.

It turned out to be jellied eel. It was one of Alcuin's least favoured dishes, which left him feeling disgruntled. Or maybe it was the whole situation with Brother Galen that unsettled him. He couldn't understand why someone who was held in such antipathy by his fellow monks could be acceptable to the abbot. Why was he happy to join them together to produce a codex?

His eyes swept down the silent rows of monks, looking for Galen. He found him at the bottom corner of the table, nearest the door. Galen was hunched over his bowl of pottage in much the same way as he hunched over his manuscripts. His left arm was drawn up tight against his chest, his hand clenched into a fist. His right hand moved the spoon from the bowl to his mouth in exactly the same rhythm as he moved his hand from inkwell to manuscript in the scriptorium. He looked neither left nor right and appeared sunk in his own world and not really listening to a reading of the rules of St Benedict.

What made Alcuin angry, though, was that a fat monk sat beside Brother Galen and ate the entire portion of jellied eel. It seemed to Alcuin that the monk had deliberately sat next to Galen with the express purpose of polishing off his food. This suspicion was further strengthened when Galen put his spoon down when his bowl was still half full. The fat monk, without even asking for permission, swapped his bowl with Galen's and drained the pottage in a couple of hefty gulps.

Alcuin was outraged and looked around the refectory to see if anybody else had noticed. It didn't look like it. All the senior monks who were at the abbot's table didn't. These occupants comprised the prior, the chamberlain, the master of the boys, the armarius and Brother Benesing, the infirmarius.

There was very little family resemblance to Galen in that hard, proud face. His tonsure only made a half-crown of white hair. A receding hairline had obliterated the rest. He had an extraordinary pair of flying bushy eyebrows, from under which his sharp eyes peered out, missing nothing.

He shot a look at his nephew, frowned as if considering a problem, then let his eyes sink back to his food in which he became apparently absorbed. Alcuin watched him through the meal and saw him shoot another worried look at Galen before they all rose for their last working period.

During the hour of silent work, Galen returned to his writing and Alcuin to his surreptitious watching. It was dimmer now as the winter sun was beginning to set and clouds had built up. So Galen was leaning much closer to the vellum to see what he was doing. Other than that, he had the same motion as before, but slower.

Alcuin wasn't surprised. It was freezing now, and his fingers had long since gone numb. By this time of the day, he stuck to the easier parts of his illuminations as it was harder to hold his brush and do intricate work.

It was so cold in the scriptorium that he could see the brothers' breath as they sighed through the last hour. Compline couldn't come soon enough, because after those prayers it was time for bed. Alcuin was already dreaming of being tucked up under his blankets where he could at least get warm.

As had become the pattern of this day, Alcuin watched Galen as they prepared for their night's rest. As was required, Galen pulled up his hood at Compline and left it there for bedtime. But, unlike the others, who wasted no time in carrying out their final ablutions, handing in their knives and then tucking themselves up under their blankets, Galen just sank onto his bed. He sat hunched over, looking dazed as the activity of the other monks filled the room.

Brother Benesing walked in, holding an earthenware mug. He looked first to Alcuin's bed and remembered that they had moved his nephew. He made his way to the still figure, leaned down and gestured with his hand that Galen should drink. Galen waved him away. But Brother Benesing shook his head, handed over the earthen mug, and watched as Galen swallowed down its contents. He stood, gave the young man's shoulder a squeeze, and went back to his infirmary.

Galen still didn't move. Around him the other monks climbed into bed and one by one snuffed out their candles. Alcuin waited, watching all the while. Finally, when the room was illuminated by only the lamp that burned through the night, Galen slowly and, it seemed, very cautiously, lay down on his side and pulled the blanket over himself.

Chapter 6

Alcuin put his hand on his stomach and belched. He felt deeply uncomfortable. His belly was gurgling like an over-full cauldron. Whatever had been in yesterday's dinner had clearly been off because Alcuin wasn't the only one suffering. He'd woken as an explosive cannonade of farts had gone off all around him and monks had made unseemly haste to the privies.

Since then the day had scarcely improved, and discreet, and not so discreet, farts and burps filled the air. If only it also warmed the scriptorium, Alcuin thought with a sigh. Instead, all it did was stink up the air.

The problem was so all-pervasive that after the twelfth man had begged him leave to go, Brother Ranig finally snapped and said that for today any man who needed the privy should just go and not bother him. As he'd left at a near run himself a few seconds later, all was explained. He looked pale when he got back, but nobody mentioned it. They were far too preoccupied with their own discomfort to care about any other man's.

Today, for the first time in the ten days that he'd been here, Alcuin felt homesick. He wasn't thinking of his mother, father and blood siblings. No, they had packed him off to Thurby on his seventh birthday, much to his own relief and that of his mother. She was a beautiful woman but incapable of loving her children, whom she ignored and relegated to the care of a nurse.

So Alcuin had grown up in a little gang of boys. A few, like him, were the sons of nobles, the others were orphans and, one assumed, the poorest of the poor. It didn't matter to them. They had been brought up by a kindly and surprisingly tolerant master of the boys. His bargain with them was that they could do as they pleased - hunt, fish and play to their hearts' content - as long as they concentrated on their lessons and tried their best when he needed them to. It worked surprisingly well. What with that, and being the only group of children in the monastery, they had formed a bond thicker than blood.

If anything had made him hesitate about taking up the offer from Yarmwick it was that he'd be pulled away from them. But it had also been their collective counsel that he should go, for it was too great an opportunity to miss, that had finally helped him decide. Today, feeling as sick as he was, Alcuin missed them more than ever.

He was surprised out of his miserable contemplation when Brother Ranig placed a gathering on his desk.

'From him,' he muttered, with a flick of his head towards Brother Galen.

'He's finished the first gathering?' Alcuin said in surprise. 'In only ten days?'

'He's quick,' Ranig muttered grudgingly, and stomped away.

Alcuin turned to Galen who he expected to be looking his way to gauge his reaction, but no, Galen had his head down and was copying steadily. Fair enough. Since the day he'd spoken to Galen about the book, they'd not spoken again. Alcuin could come up with no reason to do so, and Galen did not try to engage in conversation with him either.

In truth, Alcuin was hesitant to get too involved. He worried that Galen may well be a catamite. Even if he wasn't, he could do without everyone else's displeasure.

Still, Galen's work impressed him as he slowly leafed through the pages. It was as close to perfect as any man could get. The squares for the illuminated capitals were geometric in their accuracy, as were the perfect proportions of the text to the page and to the spaces he'd left for illustrations.

He'd also not put any markings in to guide Alcuin on what he should paint, not the shapes of the letters, not the colours, nor the themes. Alcuin assumed that was because of their conversation. Still, it was startling to be given such a free hand.

Alcuin was a naturally curious and observant man. Since he'd found out about Brother Galen, he'd watched him whenever they were in the same room. It quickly became clear that Galen was an outcast: living on the periphery of the monks' community, but never a part of it.

He never engaged in conversation. Even in the chapter house where all were free to speak, Galen didn't join in. Not that he didn't pay attention. Watching Galen as he did, Alcuin noted that he listened closely to the tales being related. It seemed, especially in the chapter house, he was absorbed into another world. It was a world of saints and their deeds, their lives and deaths and the lands in which they had lived. His face came alive then. Whatever he felt could be read as easily as one could read his script.

Alcuin noted with interest that he often seemed to find the saints' actions amusing. A brief smile twitched the corner of his mouth up at some of their oddities. At other times he looked deeply moved by the sacrifices made by the saints, and on more than one occasion he looked frankly incredulous over the miracles ascribed to these beings.

It was a dangerous thing to have such a revealing face, Alcuin thought. Perhaps it was best that most people ignored Galen.

Looking back down at Galen's manuscript, Alcuin realised that there was actually no need to ever speak to Galen again. Brother Ranig could mediate all their interactions.

He could concentrate instead on building a relationship with the other brothers here. He didn't even have to work very hard at that. Brother Anfred was the unofficial leader of a little band of brothers, all from the scriptorium, who hung out together. They were the elites of the monastery because the scriptorium brought in a vast amount of wealth. In addition, Brother Anfred was the abbot's personal scribe. The abbot's eyes were failing and he struggled to read, so now he preferred to dictate his letters, personal thoughts and philosophies to Anfred. It meant that the librarian was privy to everything of importance that happened at the abbey. Much to the disappointment of the rest of the group, he kept his knowledge locked up in his breast.

'Much like the seal of the confessional,' Anfred said on a laugh when Wearelm was pushing him for information.

The rest of the group was made up of Brothers Waerelm and Haenric, who were both copyists, and Brother Offa who was an illuminator. Brother Offa had reason to resent Alcuin because he had been the best illuminator in Yarmwick until Alcuin's arrival. But he was an easygoing man and had said with his lazy grin, 'I intend to steal all your best images and make them my own.'

Alcuin liked him for it. In fact, the only one he didn't entirely take to was Waerelm, who came across as a gossip and a busybody. But as he was an established member of the group, Alcuin had nothing to say on the matter.

Whatever they had eaten to give them all upset stomachs was causing Galen more pain than usual. It meant that he walked at a snail's pace to the chapter house after mass. He was going to be very late. He hoped it wouldn't matter. Nobody was looking particularly well, and each man was more focused on his own misery than thinking of anyone else. Besides, his place by the door would be empty. It always was.

Galen stopped dead in the doorway. The big, burly novice, Godwin, who seemed to bully all the boys, was sitting in his place. Godwin knew full well what he was doing and grinned up at Galen with a smirk on his acned face.

Galen cast a frightened, uncertain glance around the chapter house. It was full, and the abbot was watching him, waiting to begin the meeting. For a horrified moment Galen didn't know what to do. He looked back down at the novice and the boys packed around him. There was an air of anticipation about all of them. One of the smaller boys was only just holding in a snigger. Aside from that, there wasn't a single space available.

Pain grabbed his guts and bent him over nearly double. He couldn't stay standing in the doorway, he couldn't flee, so that left only one option. Galen spotted Alcuin, scowling angrily, but also, surprisingly, pushing into his neighbour to provide a gap, so Galen scurried towards him. God only knew what he would do if the monks refused to give room. But just as he arrived, Alcuin gave Haenric a sharp jab with his elbow and the gap widened.

Galen cast Alcuin a thankful glance and pushed himself into the space. That acted as a spur to Haenric. He couldn't bear to be touching Galen and he pushed the brothers on his other side hard, to force them to give more room as he hastily shuffled across.

'Let us begin,' the abbot said. 'I will keep today's meeting brief as I am aware we are all suffering the after-effects of some rotten food. Brother Thored, have you discovered what happened?'

Brother Thored, the cellarer, was in charge of the abbey's food supplies. For a man who looked after food, he was surprisingly thin. Galen had once wondered whether his lack of interest in food had been the reason that they had given him the role. Now, he just looked acutely embarrassed.

He bowed in his seat, bobbing his head up and down in apology as he said, 'It appears some of our flour has become contaminated with mould, my abbot.'

'And that flour made it into our bread yesterday, did it?'

'I'm afraid so,' Brother Thored said. 'The contamination was extensive. I've had to dispose of all of it. We will have to buy in more flour.'

'How much will that cost?' Brother Haward, the chamberlain, asked, suddenly sitting to attention.

It was his duty to make sure the abbey lived within its means, and he was zealous about it.

On another day Galen might have found the exchange interesting, but today he couldn't focus. He wrapped both arms about himself as pain rippled through him, and bit his lip to prevent a groan from escaping. Despite the fact that he felt worse than usual, he was still acutely aware of the warm bodies of the two men on either side of him. Haenric was trying to make sure that no part of him touched Galen. Alcuin seemed not to care. He was scowling at the novices, who were still watching Galen.

The boys' glee hurt Galen so deeply his heart ached along with his guts. Why had they done such a cruel thing? It looked like they had planned it all and were taking great pleasure in their victory.

It wasn't only them. Why had Brother Sledda allowed them to do what they had done? He was sitting beside the boys but acting as if he hadn't noticed a thing.

Galen could understand the boys, they were young and foolish. But their master? He should have set an example.

Galen dropped his gaze to contemplate his toes. He was burning with such shame that he couldn't even stand up to a childish bully, and he was filled with dread. What would the boys do next?

Galen was so wrapped up with that anxiety that he didn't

hear the abbot's dismissal of the company. It was only when the men around him rose that he realised the meeting was over. Usually he would wait as everyone lingered to chat.

Today was different. There was an unseemly rush for the door. Monks were forbidden to run, and Galen suspected that was the only reason they didn't. No doubt there would already be a queue at the privy.

So there was nobody left when Galen eased himself cautiously off his seat. He'd eaten even less than usual yesterday, but he still felt dreadful. He would have to head for the privy as well.

Galen stopped as he stepped into the cloister. The novices were standing in an excited huddle just ahead of him.

'Did you see?' Godwin said, practically bouncing on the spot in his triumph.

'He didn't know what to do,' the littlest novice said, chortling with glee.

Galen didn't know what to do now either. He couldn't move. He was terrified that he'd be noticed and the novices would take their game even further.

Alcuin emerged from a shadowy doorway, grabbed the ringleader by his ear and hoisted him up onto his tiptoes.

He looked furious as he said through clenched teeth, 'If you ever do that to Brother Galen again, I will tan your miserable hide. Do you understand me?'

'It was only for a jest,' Godwin whined.

'Then you aren't fit to be a monk. Shame on you to think such a thing funny. Now get out of my sight,' Alcuin said as he shoved the boy away.

Godwin took to his heels, closely followed by his friends.

Alcuin dusted off his hands, apparently satisfied. Then he looked round and his eyes met Galen's.

'I can't stand bullies,' Alcuin said with a slight smile and a nod, and he walked off in the direction of the scriptorium.

What was the meaning of that? Galen felt a mixture of relief that he wouldn't have to worry about the boys picking on him again, shame that another man had fought his battle for him, and surprise that Alcuin had even bothered to get involved.

In fact, he hadn't just got involved, he'd been angry. All that time he'd been scowling in the chapter house, Galen had thought it was because of him. Now it appeared it was because of the novices.

Galen knew he was too soft. When he'd been at home he was quick to befriend anyone willing to talk to him. He feared now that he was getting to like Alcuin far more than was safe.

Alcuin fought the feeling of discomfort for as long as he could, but by late afternoon he couldn't take it anymore. His stomach gave another painful twitch and he was seized by a powerful need to relieve himself. As he cleared the scriptorium doors, he took off at a hobble-cum-run for the privy. He was desperate and couldn't believe that, upon his breathless arrival, every door was firmly barred.

He banged loudly on each one and shouted, 'Please, whoever's in there, for God's sake hurry. I can't hold on much longer!' as he danced uncomfortably across the floor.

He heard a bolt scrape back and lunged at a door that was being opened far too slowly. He wrenched the door out of

Galen's fingers, grabbed him by the shoulder, pushed him out of the way, and bolted himself in.

He froze for a moment in the process of hitching up his robe as he spotted a couple of drops of blood on the edge of the seat. But his need was too urgent. He brushed the blood away, sat down and surrendered to exquisite release.

It was only once he was feeling more comfortable that he considered what he'd seen. Galen's face looked even paler than usual. Now that he thought about it, Galen had hit the wall when he'd pushed him out of the way. Then - was this right? - Galen had dragged his way along the wall for the second that Alcuin could still see him while shutting the door.

He felt bad about that. He'd have to go in search of Galen and apologise. He finished his ablutions just as another monk set to bellowing that everyone was taking too long. So, grinning, he left the room and looked first left, then right, for Galen. He was no longer in the corridor, but as Alcuin headed down, he spotted Galen sitting on the stairs. His knees were drawn up to his chest, his right arm was clinging to the balustrade and his left arm was pressed hard against his body.

'Galen,' Alcuin said, as he dropped down beside the monk.

Galen closed his eyes and turned his head away.

'Listen, I'm sorry I was so rough. It was a case of dire emergency, but I shouldn't have done it.'

Galen gave a quick nod but still kept his face averted. Alcuin felt helpless and wondered what to do as he glanced down the stairs and back to Galen. He stopped as his eyes were drawn to a drop of blood forming at the bottom of Galen's left fist.

'Galen, are you alright?' Alcuin said, taking hold of his hand and forcing it open. 'God's Mercy!' Alcuin gasped as he revealed a palm in which four half-moon wounds oozed blood. All around was badly bruised flesh and the scars and scabbed remains of further injuries. 'You need help!'

Galen took a shuddering breath, pulled his hand out of Alcuin's clasp, clenched it and drew it back to his body.

'Come on,' Alcuin said as he gripped Galen's elbow and lifted him gently. 'I'm taking you to the infirmary.'

Galen gasped with the pain and closed his eyes for a second before he allowed himself to be guided down the stairs. Guided wasn't quite right, as Alcuin was taking most of Galen's weight.

'For God's sake, slower,' Galen whispered.

'Sorry,' Alcuin said, now seriously alarmed.

It seemed that all the blood drained from Galen's face as Alcuin lifted him up. Alcuin now understood how somebody could be described as ashen. The greyish-white look of Galen's face was exactly that.

They walked through the cloister and out into the less orderly collection of buildings to the south of the abbey. Just behind the hall allocated to guests was the infirmary. It was another long, low, wooden building that resembled a village hall. A cluster of monks stood around the entrance, other sufferers of the food poisoning. Brother Benesing was talking to them and looked none too sympathetic.

Alcuin was considering pushing through them with Galen because he looked a lot worse than the rest, when Brother Benesing spotted him.

'Alright, go inside,' Brother Benesing said to the monks,

'Brother Wiglaf will give you something to settle your stomachs.' The other monks disposed of, Benesing hurried to Alcuin's side, took Galen by his other arm and turned them away.

'Come, help me get Galen to my house.'

'Your house?'

'I prefer to have him in my house where I can keep him under my eye night and day,' Brother Benesing said.

Alcuin was wondering whether he'd not done enough. Wasn't it better to leave Galen in his uncle's care and go back to the scriptorium? It didn't look like Brother Benesing would give him that option.

So he helped support Galen as they went round the side of the infirmary and through the gates into a walled garden. On one side of the garden path was a bed of hardy-looking herbs: rosemary and lavender mingled with sage and thyme. The other side of the path had an empty bed, tilled in readiness for the seedlings as soon as the ground was warm enough to take them.

At the end of the garden path was a small cottage. It had a bleached wooden bench against the outside wall. It was an ideal spot to sit on a sunny day as the space before the house was a south-facing sun trap. Today it was far too cold and windy.

Brother Benesing took his little group inside. It was a simple place, a single room that had two narrow beds pulled up against opposing walls. A solid oak table occupied the space in the middle of the hut. A chopping board, several pestles and mortars of varying sizes, a knife and a couple of mixing bowls littered its surface. On the side to the left of the door was a fireplace. The fire was lit and a cauldron was bubbling over it. The liquid inside was black and smelled bitter. Alcuin assumed it was medicine. Neat rows of flasks and earthenware pots filled the shelves to either side of the chimney.

'This way,' Brother Benesing said, and guided Alcuin and Galen to one of the beds. Galen sank down onto it with a sigh of relief. 'Galen are you bleeding?'

Galen gave a slight nod, far too exhausted and in too much pain to speak.

'Alright, wait,' Benesing said. 'Brother Alcuin, I'd appreciate it if you helped keep Brother Galen upright for a little longer.'

'Yes, of course,' Alcuin said. 'There was blood on the privy seat. That was why I went looking for him.'

'Indeed,' Benesing said, as he poured out a measure of a milky-looking liquid. He held it to Galen's lips and he drank it down without complaint. 'Now, Brother Alcuin, ease him down onto the bed. I'll get his legs,' Benesing said as he grasped Galen by the ankles and lifted his legs together onto the bed. He covered Galen with a blanket and said, 'Rest. I'll come back to you presently.'

Alcuin doubted that Galen heard the command. His eyes were already closed. Benesing watched Galen for a few minutes until his ragged breathing grew even and he sank into a drug-induced sleep. Then he motioned for Alcuin to follow him, and stepped out into a brisk winter wind. Alcuin didn't mind, it was better than being inside with Galen.

'Thank you for bringing Galen here. I doubt any other monk would have done the same.'

'They all think he's a catamite,' Alcuin said, and held his breath. It was rude to have brought it up to a family member, but he wanted to know the truth.

'They do.'

'Is he?' Alcuin said, and wondered how far he could push this line of questioning, considering how terse the infirmarius was being.

'I don't know,' Benesing said with quiet deliberation, as he motioned for Alcuin to sit on the wooden bench beside the door. 'Who can say that of any man when you can't look into his soul? What I can tell you is that he has never gone near a man since he came to this abbey.'

Alcuin sat down and expected Benesing to join him. Instead, he took a small curved knife out of his sleeve and set to pruning the rosemary bush closest to the door.

'He's shunned here. They aren't likely to give him the opportunity.'

'That is also true,' Benesing said, as he gathered a handful of clippings.

'Sodomy is a mortal sin. You must have had some belief in his innocence to make you plead your nephew's case.'

'I believe what happened was done against his will.'

'What did happen?'

'Nobody knows for certain. They found his bruised and battered body naked outside his father's great hall. Someone had smashed his face in–'

'That explains the broken nose.'

'Exactly. Someone had abused his body in every conceivable fashion and it was obvious to all that he'd been sodomised. His father is a proud man. He could accept many things, but not that. He took one look at Galen, comprehended what had happened, turned his back on the boy and said, "That is not my son."'

'Who is his father?' Alcuin said, not surprised by how events had unfolded.

'Ealdorman Hugh. You may have heard of him.'

Alcuin gasped, shocked by this revelation. 'He is one of the most powerful lords in the land. If he turns against you, you stand no chance.'

'I apprehend your father is also of the nobility?' Benesing said, and dropped his clippings into a shallow wicker basket by the door. He carried it with him, placed it beside the bush and returned to his pruning.

'He is, and he lives in uneasy truce, imposed by the king, with Ealdorman Hugh.' Alcuin felt on uncertain ground and wondered why he was revealing so much. 'Truth be told, there's a feud between our two families.'

'I see. That puts a different complexion on things. Will you hold to the feud?' Benesing asked, as he straightened up from his pruning and examined Alcuin from under his bushy eyebrows.

Family honour was important, so Alcuin said cautiously, 'You said Ealdorman Hugh disowned Galen. Therefore, he is no longer a part of the family against which my own is ranged. But with such a man set against him, how did Galen get here?'

'His mother used her influence to have Galen brought to me. I have tried to help the boy to the best of my ability. Sadly, I seem unable to cure him. Occasionally he improves, but just when I think he might be on the road to recovery, he suffers a relapse.'

'It might have been kinder to let him die,' Alcuin said, and took a deep breath that filled his nostrils with the rich smell of rosemary.

Benesing nodded, his eyes searching Alcuin's face. 'Galen was ever a shy boy. But he had a sweetness of disposition that endeared him to all who took the time to get to know him. Sadly, it was something his father never cared to do. He had little time for any boy who wasn't a natural-born fighter. I always thought that was a pity, for Galen had a spark of life to him that was particularly attractive.'

'He doesn't have it anymore.'

'It has been extinguished,' Benesing said with a heavy sigh, as he turned back to the pruning. 'Ever since the attack I can no longer see the Galen I knew. I just see a shell of a being that looks like my nephew.'

'Who did it?'

'That I don't know. Galen has never spoken of the matter to me or to anyone else.'

'Surely he has made his confession?'

'I assume so, but I am not his confessor and I wouldn't break his confidence if he had confessed to me.'

'No, of course not,' Alcuin said. 'What will you do now?'

'I'll continue to treat him and to pray that one day he will be fully healed.'

'Can you do nothing else?' The current solution seemed woefully inadequate to Alcuin. He also wondered why Brother Benesing kept pruning. Maybe it made the conversation easier. Or maybe he was just the kind of man who couldn't sit still.

'I don't know what else to do. It is obvious he suffered some internal injury, but I cannot divine what it was, so I can't do anything about it.'

'He must be in a great deal of pain. His left hand is a mass of injuries where he keeps digging his fingernails into the flesh.'

'Those are wounds I can treat,' Brother Benesing said.

'This is intolerable!'

Brother Benesing smiled at that and looked out across his garden as he said, 'I am glad you feel it so. Nobody else in the abbey feels that way.'

'He's an excellent scribe, Brother Benesing, how can I not admire a man who can produce such outstanding work?'

'I heard that the abbot had paired the two of you up. It has caused a certain amount of consternation.'

'My brothers have made their displeasure known.'

'And still you hold firm in your resolve. I must ask why.'

It was a question Alcuin had asked himself many times in the last ten days. Today, though, had provided him with part of his answer.

'Galen is an excellent scribe. No manuscript of mine has ever looked as good as what we will finally produce.'

'I dare say Galen could say the same about you.' Brother Benesing said, giving Alcuin's face a searching look as if he were weighing him up.

'Has he said the same to you?'

'He talks to me only marginally more than he talks to anyone else.'

'Which is to say, not at all.'

Benesing gave a great, gusty sigh. 'They ostracise him and

he hasn't the strength of will to force them to acknowledge his existence. But, impossible as it may have been for you to see it, your choosing him to be your copyist has been a bright moment in a dark life. I believe it means a lot to him.'

Alcuin wished Brother Benesing had not said that. The last thing he wanted was to feel like he owed Galen anything. It would only make him feel bad if he withdrew from him. Maybe that was exactly why Brother Benesing had said it.

'Here,' Benesing said, as he handed over his basket of rosemary clippings, 'drop this off at the kitchen for me.'

Chapter 7

As Alcuin filed out of the church on Sunday after mass, following a row of black-robed monks, he kept an eye open for Brother Benesing. He usually gathered with the senior monks clustered about the abbot. For the last couple of days, though, he hadn't been in attendance. Alcuin had searched in vain for him in the chapter house in the mornings and the refectory during dinner.

In fact, Brother Wiglaf, as the second most senior healer, had reported back during the chapter meeting on how everyone was doing after the food poisoning.

Now, nearly a week after the incident, Brother Benesing finally reappeared. He didn't look like he would hang about after mass, though. If Alcuin was to speak to him and find out how Galen was doing, this was his chance.

He thought it best to ask rather than just visit Brother Galen, for fear of what his friends might say. Not for the first time this week, he'd wondered about the wisdom of working with Galen. It wasn't just the foul rumour about him; it was also the fact that he was sickly. What use was it to have a superb scribe, a very able and fast copyist, if they constantly lost time to illness?

Alcuin was pushing his way through his friends when a hand was placed firmly on his chest, blocking him.

'Where are you going?' Anfred said.

Since he was the oldest of the little group, Alcuin owed him respect, and therefore removed Anfred's hand more gently than he might otherwise.

'I need to speak to Brother Benesing.'

'To ask about Galen, no doubt,' Waerelm said in a voice dripping with suspicion as he closed the distance to Alcuin.

'He is my scribe,' Alcuin said, surrounded by his friends now and unable to move. 'I can't progress on my codex without him.'

If there was anyone he regretted forming a friendship with, it was Waerelm. He craved attention and made sure he was always in the middle of every conversation. He was worst when it came to Galen. He didn't even bother being polite when he talked about him. He rarely actually called him Brother, as if he was making a point.

'I heard he's still feverish,' Haenric said. He was a stocky, dark man who seldom spoke. Waerelm had once joked that Haenric had taken a vow of silence.

'You're friendly with Brother Wiglaf, aren't you?' Offa said.

'We come from the same village,' Haenric said. 'He told me that Brother Benesing has his hands full with Brother Galen. He's taken a fever and is tossing and turning so much they can't settle him. Aside from that, he's so out of it he doesn't even recognise his own uncle.'

'When did you hear that?' Anfred asked.

'A couple of days ago,' Haenric said, and then lapsed back into silence.

'I hope he's improved since then.' Alcuin immediately regretted voicing his opinion out loud as it got him a sardonic look from Brothers Anfred, Offa and Haenric and a black look from Waerelm.

'You're doing yourself no favours, you know?' Anfred said, fortunately only in the tone of voice of one giving advice.

'I am aware of that,' Alcuin said. 'But it's been a week, and I am troubled. If he doesn't get better soon, I may have to move to another copyist and I don't like the idea.'

'The way you behave it's as if there are no other scribes,' Haenric said with a sad shake of his head.

Alcuin was aware that one of the scribes he'd rejected was Brother Haenric. He couldn't tell him that, even if he had to choose someone else, Haenric wouldn't be in the running. He was quick too, but it had been his script that had been the least even.

'I don't understand this desire of yours,' Waerelm said, breaking in on Alcuin's thoughts. 'If you aren't careful, you'll have people saying you're a catamite too.'

'I am not.'

'So you say,' Waerelm said, in a way that showed he had his doubts.

Alcuin scowled at him but decided against trying to defend himself. He wouldn't shift any opinions, no matter how vehement his denial.

Waerelm pushed on, despite the lack of encouragement. 'They should have let him die when he first arrived. And they should leave his fate in God's hands now. Let Him be the judge of what happens next.'

'Sometimes, Brother Waerelm, you go too far,' Anfred said.

It was just as well he stepped in, Alcuin thought, or he might have hit Waerelm. Although he was guiltily aware that he himself had said something similar to Benesing.

'Whatever you think, I still need to know how he is doing, and for that I need to speak to Brother Benesing.'

'You'd do better just saying a prayer for Galen,' Offa said. This observation surprised everyone. 'The abbot has never allowed a prayer to be offered for him at one of our masses and I know Brother Benesing has asked for that.'

'Why not?' Alcuin said.

'He doesn't say. I assume for fear that Galen is actually a sodomite.'

'Well, I will pray for him,' Alcuin said, shaking his head at the wrongness of Galen's treatment at this abbey. 'And now I am even more determined to speak to Brother Benesing.'

With that declaration, he pushed his way forcefully through the crowd of brothers who, having left the church, were now mingling in the cloister, chatting before they went their separate ways for their day of rest and contemplation.

Alcuin walked as quickly as was seemly and soon caught up with Benesing, who was ambling along. He looked tired.

'Forgive me, Brother,' Alcuin said as he tapped the infirmarius on the elbow from behind to draw his attention, and then moved past him so they could talk. 'How is Brother Galen doing?'

'He's on the mend,' Benesing said, keeping to his slow pace.

'May I visit him?' Alcuin said, and cursed his unruly tongue to have blurted out something it shouldn't have.

Brother Benesing looked him over thoughtfully and then glanced back at the mass of monks who, despite looking like they were engaged in chat, were surely all earwigging on their conversation.

'If you wish it, you may as well come now,' Benesing said.

'I heard he was feverish. Is a visit wise?'

'He has recovered from that, thank God,' Benesing said. 'He'll know you now. But he still tires easily, so bear that in mind before urging him to go back to work.'

'How did you–'

Brother Benesing shrugged and said, 'Why else would you want to see Galen?'

Alcuin nodded acceptance as he fell into step with Benesing, and they made their way out of the cloister and down the path toward Benesing's hut. Not for the first time, Alcuin wondered why he was so interested in Galen. There was no benefit in it for him.

His fellow monks already suspected him of dark things, merely for worrying about Galen's welfare. Heaven knew how they'd react if he struck up a friendship with Galen. Not that he was considering such a thing. He supposed curiosity was driving him, and a certain sense that no man, no matter how depraved, deserved the ostracism that Galen had to endure.

'Go in,' Brother Benesing said when they reached the hut. 'I'll wait in the garden.'

Alcuin nodded and stepped inside, then waited for his eyes to adjust to the dimmer light. As with the last time, the cauldron was over the fire and a fragrant steam was rising gently from it. This time it emitted a fruity smell that, added to the warmth of the fire, made the hut very pleasant. All the same, Alcuin felt nervous, and unsure of what he'd say to Brother Galen.

Galen was lying on his side, propped up on several pillows, reading a small, plainly bound book. He'd drawn his legs up, making a curve of his body. It was always the same with him, standing or lying, he kept that stoop. It seemed Galen lived permanently with pain.

'Good morning,' Alcuin said, as he sank to his haunches beside the bed. He was trying hard to pretend that what he was doing was nothing special. 'How are you doing?'

Galen's eyes flicked up to him for a moment and he looked confused. Then he sank his gaze to the floor. 'Why do you want to know?'

'Just curious, I suppose.'

It was an overly familiar gesture, but Alcuin couldn't stop himself as he took hold of Galen's bandaged left hand and turned it to look at the palm. At least the wrapping was clean, and no blood had seeped through.

A shudder passed over Galen at the contact, and he pulled away. 'I am not a catamite.'

'So I've been told. There's no need to withdraw from me.'

Galen shot him an uncertain look and said softly, 'The only one to offer me friendship in this abbey was a catamite who lost interest when he discovered I was not one.'

'I see. Well, you need not have any concerns on that front. I'm not offering you friendship. I just came to see how you're doing,' Alcuin regretted how harsh that disavowal sounded. But he had to be careful too, and make things plain.

Galen's eyelids fluttered in a confusion of thought. 'Oh,' he murmured.

'Do you think you'll be able to come back to the scriptorium soon?'

'I don't know. You must ask my uncle.'

'You at least have a friend in him, you know?' Alcuin said, trying to inject some hearty positivity into his voice.

Galen looked up again, checking that his uncle wasn't around, and said, 'We don't really talk.'

'Oh,' Alcuin said. Then, because he couldn't think of anything else, he asked, 'What are you reading?'

'Just some poems,' Galen said, and pulled the book under his blanket so that all that was visible was a rectangular shape.

'Poems? I like poetry; whose are they?'

Galen flushed deep red and murmured, 'They're... they're mine. I would write more but it takes... it takes too much concentration, especially now.'

'So you're a poet too?' Alcuin said, and Galen rose in his estimation. He looked insignificant, yet he seemed to have a wealth of talent.

'I'm just a copyist. I don't think... I wouldn't be allowed to do original work. Maybe one day I'll be given a translation, though. I'd like that.'

'Translations too? What would you translate?'

'Latin into Englisc so... so ordinary people can read the great works.'

'Do you think they want to?'

'I don't know.'

'May I look in your book?' Alcuin asked. As always, his curiosity was getting the better of him.

'It's nothing special, just my workbook,' Galen said, but he didn't resist as Alcuin eased it from between his fingers.

The book looked like it had been in Galen's possession for a long time, and was filled with Latin grammar, quotes from the Bible, and poetry, as well as, to Alcuin's delight, a lot of riddles.

'Are these also yours?' Alcuin asked, holding one out for inspection.

'Not the riddles; those I wrote down whenever I came across a new one.'

'But you haven't put in the answers.'

'I know the answers,' Galen said, sounding puzzled by Alcuin's statement.

'May I make a guess at one? I'll read it aloud,' Alcuin said, and, without waiting for permission, he read:

I rise up, powerful and wild.
Far I am driven.
Dark I sweep over the lands,
My roof made of water.
I shake the forest and break the beams of the trees.
Furious I thunder fiercely over the dark rooftops.
With havoc I burn the long hall and ravage homes.
Smoke mounts on high,
Pandemonium is victorious.
Sudden death bring I to men on my avenging path.
Tell me, wise men, learned and crafty, what am I?

'That's pretty good,' Alcuin said and considered the words. 'It sounds to me like it is describing a few things.'

Galen nodded and murmured, 'As many as the fingers on my hand, and joined together like a fist.'

'Even better,' Alcuin said, rubbing his hands together with glee. It took him a while, picking through the words and trying to turn them into an image in his mind. As he considered one option after the other, he also kept watching Galen. He seemed to be having trouble keeping awake.

'I think it's a storm,' Alcuin said, 'with wind, rain, thunder and lightning.'

'Yes,' Galen murmured, as his gaze sank to the floor. He looked exhausted, as if it was too much effort to talk.

'Oh... well I'd better go,' Alcuin said, feeling Galen's depression seeping into his heart. Really, it was none of his business, this, and he was better off keeping his distance.

He gave Brother Galen a nod of farewell that was barely noticed, never mind acknowledged, and stepped outside.

Brother Benesing was bending over double in his herb garden. As he heard Alcuin emerge, he hastily straightened up. Since it was Sunday, he wasn't supposed to be doing any work, but Alcuin spotted the handful of weeds he slipped into his voluminous sleeve.

Alcuin thought perhaps he was a good illustrator because he was observant. He could draw upon all he saw to populate his illuminations. Everyone, upon viewing his work, would say straight away that what he'd drawn was spot on, but they wouldn't have thought to put those details in themselves.

Maybe it also made him care more about what he saw. Maybe that explained why he'd visited Galen.

'Are you satisfied, now that you've seen him with your own eyes?' Benesing asked.

'It is a relief to know that he is on the mend,' Alcuin said. 'I assume he'll be returning to work soon.'

'Most likely,' Benesing said.

As he looked like he wished to be left alone so he could return to his weeding, Alcuin nodded, murmured, 'Thank you for letting me see Brother Galen,' and hurried away.

Galen lay, staring at the square of sunshine that spilled onto the floor from the open doorway, contemplating Alcuin's visit. Nobody in the monastery had ever visited him before. It left his emotions in a tumult.

This latest action of his added to everything else he'd done. Choosing Galen as his scribe, standing up for him against the novices and searching him out and bringing him to the infirmary. Any other man would merely take them as acts of kindness. But for Galen, with his reputation... What did it mean? Galen knew that just looking like a warrior, as Alcuin did, didn't exclude them from being a catamite.

A tremor of fear shook his hands and he nearly lost his grip on his book. He had two sources of dread. The first was the more primal. He feared what Alcuin might want. The second was the one that hurt more. What if he was actually a friend? No, such a thing wasn't possible. He had to make sure he never even hoped for it to be a reality.

A squeak from the garden gate pulled Galen from his contemplation of Alcuin to wonder who had come. Galen had once seen his uncle pouring boiling water over the iron hinges of his gate. So he knew that the sharp, shrill noise was deliberate and warned him of approaching people.

It made Galen anxious. People rarely came to his uncle's house, so he was probably the reason for the visit.

'Benesing, what progress from your patient?' came the voice of Abbot Dyrewine from the garden.

Galen's breath caught, and he froze. It would have been more sensible to lie down now and pretend to be asleep, but he couldn't move.

'He is making a slow recovery,' his uncle said. 'He has ceased bleeding these three days and more, but he is as weak as a newborn. I doubt he could stand up unaided yet.'

'Will he recover?' the abbot said, and sat down at the bench beside the door.

He cast a shadow against the frame of the window, but otherwise was out of sight. Galen could still hear every word, as the window was also open. His uncle believed in the restorative power of fresh air. In this he was different to most healers who kept sick rooms shut up tight lest the elves get in and spread infection.

'He has recovered before,' his uncle's voice came, along with the sound of him settling on the bench beside the abbot.

'But for how long?'

'What do you want to know, my abbot?' Benesing said, and echoed Galen's own doubts.

'I want to know whether I was a fool to make him the scribe for my star illustrator. Should I have given Alcuin someone more robust to work with?'

'I can't answer that question. Galen will go back to work this time, but I can't say that this problem of his won't recur, or whether the next time it does it won't kill him,' Benesing said.

He'd never said as much to Galen, but it was what he feared himself. It was worse to hear it from the man he relied upon to keep him alive.

'You never did get him back to full health, did you?' the abbot said, and Galen was surprised to hear regret in the man's voice.

'I'm afraid not. I fear some of his suffering resulted from my over-eagerness to get the boy back onto his feet and out working. I sent him out too soon and that may have stalled his healing and caused damage which I may now never be able to reverse.'

'Mmm,' the abbot grunted, and then there was silence. Galen held his breath, waiting, dreading to hear what the abbot said next. Part of him wanted to stuff his fingers into his ears for fear of what he might say, but he still couldn't move. 'He's the best scribe I have, Benesing. It isn't just that his hand is particularly fine. He corrects things. I've noticed that the works he's copied out contain none of the faults of spelling and errors of grammar and, much as it pains me to say it, the downright illiterate writing of the original. He turns it all into very pretty phrases.'

'I didn't know that.'

'Very few people do. Not many of my monks study the texts the way I do. He does nothing heretical, mind you. He just restores them to their correct language, placing the verb in the right place, for instance. It's most gratifying.'

'I am glad to hear that his work pleases you, my abbot.'

'Yes,' Abbot Dyrewine said, 'one day I might even give him a chance to do some translating.'

Galen stifled a gasp to hear this. The abbot liked his work! It had surprised him to be chosen as Alcuin's scribe, but to hear this, to hear that the abbot had noticed his minor corrections and approved of them. It was overwhelming.

'But you won't set him to translating yet?' His uncle's voice came in through the window, pulling Galen back into the present.

'That would not be prudent,' Dyrewine said, and his voice sounded heavy with regret. 'His situation is damnable, Benesing.'

'Why, may I ask, did you allow me to take Galen in when he first arrived?'

Now Galen's gut twisted with anxiety. This was the question he'd wondered about endlessly himself. He dreaded hearing the answer, but he was desperate to know and he held his breath waiting for the reply.

'You mean, before I knew he'd turn into one of my best scribes?' Abbot Dyrewine said, and he sounded as if he was smiling. 'Politics, my friend, why else?'

'I would have thought you'd be alienating yourself from Ealdorman Hugh by taking in his son.'

'Perhaps, yes, perhaps I am. But it is a risk worth taking.'

Was it a risk worth taking? Galen wondered. He wouldn't have thought so. His father was one of the most powerful men in the kingdom. Why risk his enmity?

'I'm afraid I don't understand,' Benesing said.

'Don't you? But your family is one of considerable influence, I would think the answer is plain to see. Now you and Galen's mother, Lady Bretana, both owe me a favour for taking Galen in.'

'All the same,' Benesing said, 'my family's influence is nothing compared to Ealdorman Hugh. Bretana was married to him precisely to keep our family safe from him, and from the encroaching Danes. That alliance worked. We have survived thanks to him. We can ill afford to alienate him.'

'I understand,' Abbot Dyrewine said. 'However, my gamble is that Ealdorman Hugh will one day be grateful to me that I kept his youngest son alive.'

'Ha! Have you ever met the man? He wasn't interested in Galen even when he was well.'

It hurt Galen to hear his uncle say so. He knew it for a fact, but it was more painful to hear it from another.

'I have observed Hugh when he and I were both playing attendance upon the king,' the abbot said.

After all his time at the abbey, Galen was aware that the abbot met with the king whenever he did his rounds of the country, maintaining his subjects' loyalty and keeping his ealdormen subservient and away from each other's throats. So the fact that the abbot had met his father many times came as no surprise.

'What did you make of Ealdorman Hugh?'

'He is more of a thinker than most warriors, although he rarely demonstrates that. Most of the time he uses force to get his own way.'

'So what makes you think he is more strategic than a mere bully?'

'Because he knows exactly where to push to gain the victory he wants. He doesn't just roar and fight any who come at him. He is powerful and ruthless but, most significantly, effective.'

'Unlike his bosom companion,' Benesing said.

'I assume you are referring to Septimus the Red.'

To hear the man's name mentioned after so many years

sent a tremor of fear through Galen. Now, more than ever, he wanted to pull the blanket over his head and blot out this conversation, but still he remained motionless and his treacherous ears strained to hear.

'I am referring to Septimus,' Benesing said dryly. 'He and Hugh are closer than brothers. And on the battlefield they are a formidable pair. Hugh is already a head taller than most men and Septimus is a half head taller than him.'

'With his hair the colour of melting iron, he is a striking fellow.'

'He has a fiery temper to match it. I never understood what Hugh saw in him,' Benesing said. 'He's loud and uncouth and gets roaring drunk at every meal.'

'Perhaps it is his family connections. His older brother, Uictred, is a confidant of the king, after all.'

'I suppose that is true. And as you say, Hugh is a canny operator. I still don't see the advantage you get by keeping Galen here.'

'Because, one day, Ealdorman Hugh may regret what he did.'

'What on earth makes you think he'll regret anything? It isn't in his nature to do that,' Benesing said with a harsh laugh.

Much as it pained him, Galen was of the same opinion as his uncle. Ealdorman Hugh never changed his mind. He was a clever, tough, uncompromising man. Galen had seen often enough in his father's hall, that once he took against someone, there was no overcoming it.

'Even though sodomy is a mortal sin, Ealdorman Hugh didn't have his son put to death,' came the abbot's voice through the window. It was filled with calm and certainty. 'Instead, he disowned Galen. When he realises his mistake, he may come and see me.'

'Mistake?' Benesing said. 'You don't know Hugh. Besides, don't you fear what might happen if the church learns you're harbouring a catamite?'

The abbot laughed at that, which surprised Galen. It was the last thing he expected of such a serious question.

'Do you really think we are the only ones to have catamites in our midst?'

Benesing took such a sharp intake of breath that even Galen heard it, and it reflected his own surprise.

'This is dangerous talk.'

'And besides the point,' Abbot Dyrewine said. 'Your nephew's behaviour has been blameless since he arrived at my abbey. I will do what I can to keep him. So tell me, what does he need to enable him to go back to work?'

It stunned Galen to hear what the abbot really thought. The questions his uncle had asked were the same that had tormented him since his arrival. The answers were the furthest from what he'd pessimistically assumed. He'd always thought the abbot was the antithesis of a spiritual man, he was just so practical. Galen had never been more grateful for that than he was now.

'He must rest as much as possible,' Benesing said. 'It would be best that he only walks to wherever is strictly necessary: the dormitory, the refectory and the scriptorium, nowhere else.'

'The church?'

'He must remain where he is when the others go to the

Divine Office. Which means he stays in bed for the prayers during the night and the morning, and in the scriptorium the rest of the time.'

'That won't make him very popular.'

'He could scarcely be less popular,' Benesing said.

'Indeed,' Abbot Dyrewine said, and his voice indicated that he wasn't best pleased with Benesing's comment. 'Tell me, why did Brother Alcuin visit him?'

'I honestly don't know. I've tried to warn him off, but he pays me no heed.'

'Leave him,' Abbot Dyrewine said, surprising Galen again. 'And as for your nephew, when he is ready he may return to his duties in the manner you recommend until you deem him well enough to go back to a full part of life in the community.'

'Thank you,' Benesing said. 'I hope that this time Galen will heal better.'

Galen barely heard the abbot's murmured farewell and the shriek of the gate as he left. Alcuin's visit had been surprising enough. The abbot's was even more of a revelation. He'd learned so much that he needed time to process it and truly understand. But now he was desperately tired. He shifted down in the bed, pulled the covers over his head and surrendered himself to sleep.

Chapter 3

Galen slipped into the scriptorium and made his way to the armarius's desk. He stopped a couple of steps from the dais and gave a quick, nervous bow.

'Oh, so you're back, are you?' Brother Ranig said.

Alcuin looked up at the sound of Ranig's voice, spotted Galen and smiled a pleased greeting. It surprised a flicker of a smile from Galen, who hastily looked back down at his toes, flushing in confusion at his own reaction.

'Go back to your desk,' Ranig said impatiently. 'I'll bring your manuscript.'

Galen gave a quick nod and kept his eyes on the floor. He didn't risk making eye contact again with Alcuin as he made his slow way to his desk. He gingerly got up onto his high seat with his curled-over hunch that caused him the least pain.

At least in the scriptorium he had something to occupy himself with. Lying in his uncle's bed, in his uncle's house, was never very comfortable. His uncle enjoyed being alone and didn't like having his space invaded. He was always perfectly polite, but not encouraging.

Galen found his mind drifting to home and to his mother and sisters. He missed them dreadfully. A tear slipped down his face and he hastily dabbed it away. Heaven help him if anyone noticed it here.

He reached up to the codex on Saint Cuthbert and flicked the pages over to the place he'd copied to. It was odd that the armarius had removed the book. Usually it was just left on the stand till he got back.

He forced himself to pay attention to the words on the page. It was difficult. Now that he'd thought of them, his mother and sisters occupied his mind. It was best that they didn't. That way lay far too much misery, because there was no going back.

He had a lot of work to do, anyway. He regretted that his illness had delayed the production of the codex. The abbot no doubt wanted it ready as soon as possible. He was an energetic and impatient man.

Alcuin, too, must nearly have finished illustrating the first gathering. After all, Galen had been away for nearly two weeks. That said, Alcuin's work was very detailed, so maybe he was still busy. Galen didn't dare look up to try to guess what Alcuin was working on. He didn't understand him.

He still couldn't work out why he'd visited him when he was ill. Why was he interested in such a fallen creature? It left Galen feeling uneasy about him.

That was another thought to push away and not dwell on. Galen forced himself to concentrate on his writing. Fortunately, that was easy. The Venerable Bede's command of Latin was a joy to work with, and his way of detailing the facts was equally masterful.

Galen became so absorbed in the manuscript that he scarcely noticed when the bells rang for the holy offices and the other monks filed away. Nor did he pay them any attention when they returned. The difference between their whoops to be freed from their desks as they left, and their groans to return and take up their pens, also barely penetrated.

The only thing he noticed was that it was getting harder to see his own writing. Galen finally looked up, rubbing his tired eyes, and gazed out of the window. It was late afternoon. The sun was low in the sky and sending out rays that warmed the bottom of a fine layer of fluffy cloud.

'It's looking good,' a voice said right beside him that made Galen jump.

He turned to find Alcuin looking down at the text with the sharp expression of an expert making an accurate appraisal of the work.

Galen gave a quick nod and double-checked the black letters arranged in perfect ranks down the page, looking for errors.

'And I see you have a glove protecting your left hand,' Alcuin said of the fingerless, black leather glove Galen's fingers were digging into.

'My uncle's doing,' Galen murmured.

'Does it work?'

Galen gave a non-committal shrug and glanced at Alcuin's face and away again. 'Your friends are waiting for you.'

'I know,' Alcuin said. 'It will do them no harm.'

His smile was mirrored briefly in Galen's eyes, then he said, 'You should go.'

And Alcuin did. At least he gave a polite farewell as he took his leave, but he didn't hang about. As usual, that left Galen with mixed feelings. He didn't know if he could trust Alcuin. Sometimes he was friendly and sometimes he behaved as though Galen didn't exist.

In the week that followed, Alcuin neither approached nor spoke to Galen. Galen, for his part, didn't try to gain his attention either. There would be no point, especially since he'd never been good at thrusting himself into other people's orbits.

It also relieved Galen that he could stay in bed these days when everybody else got up for Nocturns in the middle of the night. He rose for Prime, then made his way, trailing behind the rest of the brothers, to the scriptorium where he stayed all the way through Terce, Sext and Nones, when the rest of the brothers went to prayer. He only rose for dinner, Vespers and then bed, where he remained while the rest went to Compline. As far as he was aware, nobody had explained this change to the brothers, but, as neither the armarius nor the chamberlain said anything to Galen about it, he assumed they knew the abbot sanctioned his absence.

Galen felt a lot better from his rest. The arrival of spring may also have had some impact. It was no longer bitterly cold in the scriptorium. What with that, and the gloves his uncle had got him, at least his fingers didn't ache. His spirits had revived so much that he looked forward to dinner for the first time in a long time. He hoped Brother Tostig would at least not hog all the supplemental food. Today he expected it would be cheese, and he was rather partial to cheese.

Despite his hopes, the vast bulk of Brother Tostig was the

first thing to meet Galen's eyes when he arrived in the refectory. Galen was about to slide onto the bench beside him when Brother Alcuin stepped up to Tostig, tapped him on the shoulder and showed with a flick of his head that the fat man had to move.

If they'd been allowed to speak in the refectory, Galen suspected Brother Tostig might have objected, although Brother Alcuin's smile conveyed that he was determined and wouldn't back down. As Tostig couldn't speak, he had very little choice but to obey and slide further down the bench, but he gave Alcuin an unforgiving glare. Alcuin's smile broadened in triumph and he turned to grin at Galen as he shifted down the bench sufficiently to make space.

Galen gave him a startled look and wondered what he was up to now. Galen felt so uncomfortable about this turn of events that he just stared hard at his bowl and felt an embarrassed flush suffusing his cheeks. Since there wasn't a thing he could do about Brother Alcuin, he switched his attention to the monks who were working their way along the table, filling each brother's bowl.

He didn't raise his eyes again, but he was acutely aware of Alcuin's presence. And he knew his body was giving him away too. He was too stiff, and his hand moved in quick jerks as he ate, reflecting his inner disquiet.

If Alcuin did notice, he gave no sign of it. Instead, he cut the pale yellow circle of cheese they had placed between them exactly in half, and started eating his share. Despite really wanting the cheese, Galen was tempted to leave it on the plate. But that felt foolish and pointless, especially after he'd been so looking forward to it.

When the meal ended, Galen stayed where he was, as he always did, waiting for everyone else to pile out of the refectory.

Alcuin stood with all of them, but ignored his friends' calls from outside for him to join them and said, 'You go ahead. I'll see you in the scriptorium.'

Galen flicked him a quick, curious look upon hearing him, but simply rose from the table and wordlessly made his way out of the refectory.

'Aren't you going to say anything?' Alcuin said.

'What do you want? Thanks?' Galen said, breathless at his own audacity.

Alcuin gave him an astonished look for a moment, then a crack of laughter burst from him. 'I suppose I deserved that.'

'You can't help me and you only harm yourself. You'd do better to leave me alone.'

'I know, but I seem to be an odd fellow. I want to make my own choices.'

Galen gave a slight, thoughtful nod. He supposed Alcuin was right.

'You agree!' Alcuin said with a surprised laugh. 'I knew there was something more to you.'

Galen gave him an alarmed look and shook his head quickly, trying to deny Alcuin's logic. He also tried to speed up, to put an end to this disastrous conversation. Alcuin was a golden man, chosen by the Almighty to have a brilliant talent. He was destined to stride through life, happy and successful. No man with all that Alcuin had could be interested in a tainted nobody.

His interest, that had been tepid so far, could wane as

quickly as it had waxed. How would Galen feel then? How would he feel if he unlocked his heart from its deep, defensive cell and believed he had a friend, only for Alcuin to back away? For him to regret his unthinking offer of friendship and to turn cold. Galen couldn't bear it if that happened.

Still, he couldn't push Alcuin away either. For when they reached the scriptorium and Alcuin gave him a friendly nod of farewell, he didn't repulse him. All he managed was a quick nod. Although he resisted looking up into those sympathetic, laughing blue eyes.

Chapter 9

Galen's rejection stung Alcuin. As he rose from his bed, went for his ablutions, made his way to the church, washed his hands in the stone basin along with a row of brother monks, and then filed into the choir, he burned over what had happened after dinner the previous day. He couldn't concentrate as the monks started chanting.

He'd gone out of his way to be friendly, and was Brother Galen grateful? On the contrary, he'd asked exactly the wrong question. Or was it the right one? Alcuin guessed the uncomfortable night he'd spent tossing and turning was exactly because Galen had asked him what he was doing. Did he want thanks? Was he that shallow?

No, it was in his nature to be friendly. He hated to see people being excluded. When he was a boy, he was always the first to invite any orphan, freshly arrived at the monastery, to join in with their play.

He also believed in fairness above all else. If a man was a part of the abbey, they should treat him as an equal member. Just as within a company of thanes, each man was treated with respect and expected to do his all in battle to support his brothers. It was the way the world worked.

Galen was no exception, and he did his part. He never shirked his responsibilities and his work was of the highest quality. But nobody spoke to him. Brother Ranig was openly hostile towards him. Brother Tostig stole his food, and the novices thought it grand sport to pick on him.

It was wrong, and Alcuin didn't like it. He supposed that was why he went against opinion and tried to be friendly. Did Galen realise how much of a risk he was taking? Yes, of course Galen knew the risk. Which was precisely why he'd told Alcuin that he'd be hurting himself.

It was tough to be rejected though. Especially when he considered who'd done the rejecting. The one person who could really use a friend had told him to stay away. He was trying to work out whether he would, when he got a sharp elbow in his ribs. He looked up to find Brother Offa glaring at him meaningfully. Alcuin realised he'd stopped chanting, gave Offa an apologetic grimace, and turned his attention back to his prayers.

The morning didn't improve much. During the silent working period in the scriptorium, several of his fellow monks were glaring at him. The anger at him stepping out of the unwritten rule to ostracise Galen was so strong that Alcuin half expected it to be brought up at the chapter house meeting. Fortunately, it wasn't, although he received a succession of disapproving shakes of the head from the elder monks.

The moment they were back at the scriptorium and able to talk, Brother Ranig made a beeline for Alcuin's desk.

'Do you have any idea how stupid you're being?' the armarius said in a fierce undertone.

Alcuin glanced over at Galen to see whether he was listening. As always, it was impossible to tell. He had his head down and was writing steadily.

'I'm sorry, Brother.'

It burned Alcuin to make an apology when he'd done nothing wrong. But it was the quickest and easiest way to bring this scolding to an end. The last thing he needed was a scene.

'You will bring ruin upon yourself and shame upon the abbey,' Brother Ranig snapped. 'At least consider the abbot when you are tempted to do foolish things. How will he feel if you dishonour us?'

'The abbot accepted him,' Alcuin muttered, and instantly regretted it as Ranig looked like he might explode to have been so defied.

Galen might not look like he was hearing any of this, but the other brothers weren't being as subtle. All of their pens had stopped moving, and some had even looked up, watching Alcuin and Ranig. The armarius must have noticed that the only sound in the room now was the faint scratch, scratch, scratch of Galen's solitary pen.

'Get back to work!' Brother Ranig snarled as he glared at the rest of the monks.

They hastily ducked their heads and started writing. With a final venomous look of warning to Alcuin, Brother Ranig stomped over to his desk and began going through his records of vellum, ink and paints, flicking the pages noisily.

Alcuin's scolding continued when his friends huddled

round him, walking way too close, as they made their way to the church for the prayers of Sext.

'What were you thinking, Alcuin?' Waerelm said, his voice angry and sharp.

'About what?' Alcuin said perversely, because he didn't need to be told, but he was trying to delay the inevitable.

'That damned Galen, you'll share his taint if you stick so close to him.'

'I will do no such thing.' Alcuin's anger rose to a fiery rage to be taken to task again, as if his own doubts weren't sufficient. But he kept his voice low.

'You're wrong,' Anfred said, ever the voice of reason. 'There is far too much stigma attached to Galen for you to approach him and still maintain your good reputation.'

'He isn't unclean, you're all making a mistake.'

'The devil could ever make us believe that which is not,' Brother Offa said piously.

'You can't lay this at the devil's door,' Alcuin said. 'And you have no right to judge Galen. He is more honourable than the lot of you, for he knows what he is and what he is not. And he knows that amongst you walks a brother who has tried to force his attentions onto Galen when he suspected he would reciprocate.'

'Did he tell you this?' Waerelm snapped, an angry scowl on his brow.

'He did.'

'Did he tell you who it was?'

'He named no names.'

'Then he was lying,' Waerelm said, his face so red with anger that a blood vessel throbbed at his temple and spit flew from his lips even while he kept his voice low enough not to be overheard by the other monks.

They couldn't have failed to notice that there was a low-voiced argument going on, though. So Alcuin tried to calm down and keep his voice sounding like he was just chatting.

'I see no reason Galen would lie. Nor do I see why you have any cause to be as angry as you are.'

'Because I'm your friend and I'm trying to protect you, and all you can think about is a damned sodomite!'

'Peace!' Anfred whispered. 'We are nearly in the church. Calm yourself, Waerelm.'

Waerelm gave him a venomous look, but bit back what he was about to say. Alcuin was thankful for that at least, and more shaken than he cared to show. He'd never in his life felt such a burden of censure as he was now having to endure. If this was how it felt to face a morning of displeasure, how much worse to face years of it, like Galen. Still, he couldn't endure an entire day of it, never mind years. He'd have to keep his distance, at least till this foolishness wore off.

If Alcuin hadn't already known that Galen's ostracism was complete, he would have regretted his decision and the distance it created between Galen and the rest of them. But as it was, he'd realised that there was nothing he could do. So he merely hoped that Galen would benefit from the rest he was getting and that it would translate into some healing, or, at the very least, no further deterioration in his condition.

It seemed it was doing him some good. He didn't look as tired these days, although his stoop and his slow gait remained unchanged.

Chapter 10

Sundays were when Galen felt his isolation most acutely because it was the day of rest when each man could contemplate God and His works in his own personal way. This turned quite social, with the monks gathering in little groups to pray, or simply to sit in silence together.

In winter, those gatherings often took place in the warming room. It was the only space, other than the kitchen and the infirmary, that had a fireplace. Galen rarely went there. He wasn't welcome and the looks and whispered asides the monks made while glaring at him were sufficient to drive him away. It was only when the fiercest cold of winter gripped the abbey that Galen dared make the attempt.

Today was one of those cold, blustery spring days where the fire of the warming room would be a particular draw. No doubt it was full of brothers. The thought made Galen shudder.

His usual refuge on a Sunday was the church. There was a dark corner of the Lady Chapel where he could kneel without being noticed. As the space was small, no other man could fit. So if someone appeared intending to pray there, they would hastily retreat at the sight of Galen.

The Lady Chapel was Galen's favourite spot in the whole abbey, not just for the quiet and the serenity of the statue of Mary who smiled down at everyone, her arms open by her side in a gesture of welcome, but because of the altar cloth. It had come from his hometown. It had taken well over a year to design and plan it, then another year to create it. Fabrics had been ordered from around the country, but they had woven most of the sky blue cloth from wool sheared from his father's own sheep, dyed by the local dyer and woven by the women of their burh.

It had been a community effort, but his mother and sisters had done the final bit, the embroidery. When Galen contemplated the altar cloth, with its metallic silver thread creating an intricate floral pattern, it took him back to the comfortable hours he'd spent in the women's room, chatting and laughing and keeping everybody entertained with poems, stories and riddles while they worked.

Just thinking about that now made tears prick at his eyes. No, today he couldn't bear to be reminded of all that he'd lost. Today he desperately needed some company and there was only one person he could go to for that.

So after mass, and after the church had emptied of all but the few men who intended to remain there to pray, Galen made his way through the cloister, past the guest house and the infirmary and into his uncle's garden. The shriek of the gate attracted no attention, however, for the garden was empty and the cottage door shut. His uncle wasn't there.

Galen stood for a moment, wondering what to do next. The walk had taxed him, so he decided to sit for a while on the little bench by the door. At least the walls of the herb garden kept the worst of the wind away. The clouds were also intermittent, so every now and then he was bathed in warming sunshine. It brought a peace of sorts with it.

Galen looked out at the garden where fresh, green spring shoots were emerging from the ground. In the established half of the garden, the herbs were covered in tiny, tight purple buds. It would have been good if he could merely concentrate on the garden, but Galen's mind kept drifting to the scene in the scriptorium the day before.

Alcuin had been taken to task by Brother Ranig and everybody had listened in. A scolding from his friends had followed that. Galen wasn't surprised, but it pained him to know that Alcuin's troubles were because of him.

No matter how much he tried to make his writing perfect, so that Alcuin didn't regret his decision of choosing Galen for his scribe, he doubted it would help. He wished with all his heart that God would send an angel to the abbey to fix this whole mess. But he was no saint, and therefore unlikely to ever meet an angel. Angels were for the likes of Saint Cuthbert.

Galen had just finished the second chapter of the codex where an angel had appeared before Saint Cuthbert and healed his painfully swollen knee. Galen liked that the angel had been eminently sensible. He hadn't merely touched the knee and made it all better, he'd recommended a poultice of wheat flour and water be applied twice daily, and that had brought the inflammation down.

If only some divine presence could provide the cure for his pain too, Galen thought. He sent up a hasty prayer to God, apologising for always asking the same thing and for hoping for something he clearly didn't deserve.

He might have enlarged upon this when the gate squeaked, and his uncle stepped into the garden. He looked preoccupied and at first didn't notice Galen. But when he looked up, an indefinable, less-than-pleased expression flickered across his face and was banished.

'Galen, are you ill?' Benesing said as he came briskly towards his nephew.

'No,' Galen said, embarrassed, and sorry he'd intruded on his uncle when he wished to be alone.

'Then what is it?' Benesing said, as irritation furrowed his brow.

'I want... I just want to talk!' Galen said, and realised he sounded pathetic.

'Talk about what? Really, Galen, I'm busy, I have a lot to do.'

He shouldn't have come, Galen realised. He nodded and pushed himself onto his feet.

'I'll go then.'

'No, wait.' Benesing looked Galen over from top to bottom, sighed and said, 'Come inside. I have a tolerable plum wine you can help me drink.'

Galen was torn now, between needing company and not wanting to be a burden to his uncle. But as Benesing had stepped into his hut, he decided it was best to do as he'd been ordered.

'Sit. You look like you could use some extra food. Do you

eat everything they give you?' Benesing said, giving Galen another sharp, appraising stare.

'No.'

'You should. Especially after you've been so ill for so long. You need to build up your strength. I should have told you that when you left my house.'

Galen nodded. Now that he was here, he couldn't think of anything to say. Still, it was a comfort to have somebody bossing him around. It might be brusque, but it was how his uncle showed his concern.

'Has young Alcuin repented of making you a friend?' Benesing asked, as he put down a couple of glasses with a snap.

Galen's head jerked up, and he gave his uncle an alarmed look, before following it with a brief nod.

'I dare say the others worked on him.' Benesing poured out the wine, a thick, syrupy, dark purple liquid, handed a glass to Galen and said, 'Drink up, that too will do you good.'

Galen wasn't so sure. He got tipsy very easily. Then again, wine often brought oblivion and he would welcome that today. So he took a sip and concentrated on the sticky, sweet, heavily plummy liquid that he rolled around his tongue, diluting it with saliva before he swallowed. Then his head sank again, and he gazed at the smooth, bleached wood of his uncle's table.

He sensed, rather than saw, his uncle first stoke up his fire, then rummage around in the low cupboard beside the fireplace. He emerged with a heavy rye loaf from which he cut a few slices and pushed a couple across the table.

Galen picked up the bread absently, twisting it back and

forth in his hands as if to snap it in two, and said, 'Do you ever... hear from my mother?'

He didn't know why he'd asked that, except that he really needed to find out. In the years he'd been at the abbey, he'd never had the courage to mention his family, and his uncle had not said a word about them either. Galen flicked a quick, anxious look at Benesing from under his brows and waited, barely able to breathe, so scared was he of the reply.

'I wrote to your mother once I knew you'd live. I sent her a second letter after they accepted you into the order to let her know you'd become a scribe. She was always pleased to hear you were doing alright.'

'Did she... did she send any messages for me?'

'If she had, I would have relayed them.'

Galen's gaze sank back to the floor, and he gave a slight nod. It didn't surprise him, but for the second time today he had to fight back tears.

'She's in a difficult position. She wouldn't have been able to write freely,' Benesing said, apparently trying to soften the blow he'd delivered his nephew.

Galen put down his glass of wine, wrapped his arms around himself and rocked slowly forward, his eyes shut tight, fighting not to show how heartbroken he was. Try as he might, he couldn't control his heavy breathing, and his eyelids twitched as he fought to bring his emotions under control again.

He wasn't sure how much time passed before Benesing said, 'Is life growing too hard to bear, Galen?'

'I miss them,' he managed to whisper.

'All of them?'

'My mother... my sisters.'

'Not your father or brothers?'

Galen forced himself to open his eyes and said, 'I never pleased my father. He wanted sons who were noble warriors. I would never be that.'

'No, the plan was always for you to be a monk and you got what you wished for.'

'No,' Galen said sadly. 'I hoped... I hoped when I became a monk I'd finally find men I could talk to. Men who venerated thought and learning as much as my brothers loved hunting and sports and fighting.'

'Maybe one day they'll come round,' Benesing said.

Galen knew that his uncle understood that he had always longed to share his thoughts. He had always known how difficult it was for a shy young Galen in a household of men of action, for he had been to visit once or twice. At the time, he'd promised Galen that life would be better for him at the abbey.

'Maybe there is still hope for that. Maybe you could move to another abbey, one where the brothers know nothing of your past. You could have a fresh start.'

Galen looked up in astonishment, and hope sprang into his heart, flickered, then died. 'No, I need to stay here, near to you, just in case...'

'That might not always be necessary. In time you may well heal and be able to travel.'

Galen nodded. He tried to smile, to show that the suggestion had comforted him, but he doubted he managed more than a wry grimace. 'I should go,' he muttered, and hurried away. His uncle made no attempt to stop him.

Chapter 11

alen finished another chapter on the life of Saint Cuthbert that fitted gratifyingly neatly into the eight-page gathering. It had been a fascinating read, telling as it did of a storm at sea that threatened to shipwreck a fleet of boats. Saint Cuthbert had sent earnest prayers up to heaven, begging God for help. Miraculously, the wind eased and drove the ships safely up onto the shore by his monastery.

Galen was out of gatherings now, so he looked to Brother Ranig. He was engrossed in his work. Galen bit his bottom lip and tried to decide what to do. If he waited to be noticed, Ranig would tell him off for being lazy and sitting around when he should have been working. He couldn't shout for his attention because then everyone would look at him. That left him with only one choice.

He got gingerly out of his desk and made his way to the front of the scriptorium. He stopped at the foot of the dais upon which Brother Ranig's desk sat, and waited.

'What?' Brother Ranig snapped as he noticed Galen.

'I've got another gathering for Brother Alcuin,' Galen murmured, feeling foolish that he'd done this. He should have just waited for Ranig to come to him. Maybe he'd done it to gain Alcuin's attention.

Alcuin was working at the desk beside Ranig, but he didn't raise his head at Galen's approach. Galen didn't really expect him to, but he had hoped that he would. When Alcuin made no sign that he'd been noticed, Galen's heart sank again.

Evidently, Alcuin had repented of his earlier actions. Like a fool, Galen had let himself believe he might be a friend. It was especially stupid after he'd told Alcuin to stay away. All the same, he'd allowed Alcuin's friendliness to get to him.

Galen held desperately onto the fast-fading dream of friendship. But as the days passed, it became clear that Alcuin had ranged himself with the rest of the abbey. He was content to allow the armarius to relay any messages necessary for completion of the manuscript. That faint lightening of Galen's spirit sank into despair again.

Still, there was no point in dwelling on the misery, although it did make him return to his uncle's words about moving to another abbey. The more he considered it, the more the idea grew. Could he really go somewhere else? Somewhere nobody knew him? Somewhere that nobody knew what had happened to him?

The abbot had invited Alcuin and several other monks to join them at Yarmwick. He'd also sent a number of monks to other monasteries during the time Galen had been there. Would he allow Galen to do the same?

Could he arrive as a simple monk? A letter of introduction from the abbot, with possibly a kind word about his abilities as a scribe, and nothing more, clutched in his hand? Somewhere even his father and his hangers-on wouldn't find? Could he leave the loneliness and the dread behind?

He'd pushed the fear down. It had been a couple of years now, and nobody from home had come for him. Perhaps because his uncle was here. Perhaps because the man who attacked him knew that to come back for him would destroy his own cover and bring his father's gaze upon him.

But in the blackest moments of night, when all reason fled, fear stole an icy grip around Galen's heart. It was all too easy to believe, then, that the man who had brought down all this misery on Galen could come after him. And this time he'd silence him as he'd failed to do the first time.

Galen froze, his quill hovering over the inkhorn. Someone was standing beside him. Someone trying to be quiet, but with his breath coming just a little too fast and high. Galen slowly turned around and registered that he was alone except for Waerelm standing beside him with a crazed look in his eyes.

Waerelm grabbed him by the shoulders and pulled him into an embrace, his lips locked hard onto Galen's mouth. A shudder of disgust ran through Galen. He turned his head and tried to pull free from Waerelm's iron grip.

'I will make you mine!' Waerelm gasped and came at Galen for a second kiss.

'No!' Galen shouted, and with every ounce of his strength he pushed against Waerelm, but he could do little more than get his face away. The man was far stronger than he was. It tipped Galen back into nightmare.

Waerelm hung on, pulling at Galen's robes. The desk

rocked violently back and forth and pens tumbled to the floor.

'You can struggle all you like,' Waerelm said. 'I have twice your strength, and this time I won't listen to your pitiful words. I know what you want from Alcuin, but you won't have it. You're mine, do you hear me?'

'In God's name, let me go!' Galen cried, and panic gave him the strength to wrench himself free. It was so sudden and unexpected that he lost his balance and fell backwards away from Waerelm, dragging the desk with him. It fell on top of him with a crash. Vellum pages fluttered, the inkhorns flew free and bounced across the floor. Ink splashed everywhere.

'Come here,' Waerelm shouted, his enraged red face twisted in a fearsome scowl as he reached through the desk to get at Galen lying stunned on the floor.

'No!' Galen gasped, and snatched up his penknife which had landed beside him.

Waerelm laughed as he grabbed hold of Galen's habit and pulled.

Galen kicked against him and twisted around, his knife poised over Waerelm's hand. This could not happen again. Not here.

'Galen, no!' Alcuin shouted, appearing at the door.

The other monks collided into him as they tumbled into the room.

Galen couldn't stop himself. He stabbed Waerelm's arm in a frenzy, puncturing it over and over in a panic that wouldn't subside.

'Get him!' somebody shouted, and the screaming Waerelm was dragged back by a flurry of monks.

Galen dropped the knife and curled into a ball of agony. He

was done for now, he thought, his breath coming in tight, tearful gasps.

'Are you alright?' Alcuin asked, as he pushed the desk out of the way and hurried around it to Galen's side.

Galen stared at him in wide-eyed terror and shook his head. How could he possibly be alright?

'Shall I help you to the infirmary?'

'I don't need your help.'

Galen was terrified and in so much pain that he could only speak through gritted teeth as he clawed his way up the wall. He clung grimly to the pillar of the window and pulled himself upright.

'What is the meaning of this?' Brother Ranig shouted as he ran into the scriptorium and took in the scene of devastation. 'What have you done to my scriptorium? What have you done to Alcuin's manuscript?' he cried, as he picked up the pile of vellum. The edges were sodden with spilled ink and a sprinkling of blood.

'Nothing,' Galen whispered frantically. Dear God, everything was going wrong, just like last time. 'I did nothing.'

'Don't believe him!' Waerelm screamed, clutching at his bleeding arm. 'He tried to rape me!'

Galen staggered backward, shocked that Waerelm would accuse him. 'I did nothing,' he said, but his voice shook and he knew he sounded uncertain.

'Who are you going to believe? Me or a sodomite?' Waerelm shouted.

'What is going on here?' the abbot said, dangerously quietly, as he stepped into the room.

'That accursed sodomite tried to rape me and when I resisted, he stabbed me,' Waerelm said, waving his bloodied arm wildly at Galen.

'No,' Galen whispered. 'No,' as his eyes flicked desperately from one man to the other and saw them all withdrawing.

'It's a lie,' Alcuin said. 'When I came into the scriptorium, Galen was under the desk fighting for his life and Brother Waerelm was trying to drag him out.'

The abbot's face set like stone as his gaze travelled from Alcuin to Galen and finally came to rest on Waerelm's red and panting face. 'Take Brother Waerelm to the infirmary and have his arm seen to.'

'My abbot, I swear I was the one who was attacked,' Waerelm said.

'I will deal with you both later,' the abbot snapped. 'Now take Brother Waerelm to the infirmary.'

The group of monks that had grabbed onto Brother Waerelm, Brother Anfred amongst them, turned the raving monk away and hustled him out of the scriptorium.

'Now you, Alcuin!' Abbot Dyrewine said.

'Yes, sir?' Alcuin said with a bow.

'Take Brother Galen straight to Brother Benesing's hut. Don't bother with the infirmary. It looks like Galen has taken considerable hurt.'

'I will do that, but I have to emphasise, Brother Galen didn't–'

'No!' Abbot Dyrewine roared. 'No more talk, take him away.'

Galen stood, hanging onto the pillar, paralysed. Panic filled his heart as he gazed at the abbot. Alcuin put his arm firmly round his waist and propelled him forward.

The movement shook Galen out of the numb trance he'd fallen into and he muttered, 'I can walk.'

'Trembling the way you are?' Alcuin said with a wry smile. 'You'll shake yourself clear off your feet.'

'I don't need your help!' Galen snapped. It was perverse, but he couldn't accept help from Alcuin. Why should he? Especially if Alcuin went back to shunning him.

'Alright,' Alcuin said, and let go.

Galen took one shaky step, determined that he could do this on his own, even though the pain made it difficult to see, let alone walk. With monumental effort, he swung the next leg forward. It caved in and he fell onto one knee. He put both hands on the floor as he struggled to push himself up again. He was dimly aware that a circle of monks was watching him, but it mattered less than it usually did.

'Pride is a sin, Brother Galen,' the abbot said. 'Now you swallow it and let Brother Alcuin take you to your uncle.' With that, he spun about and marched off.

Alcuin hoisted Galen gently to his feet and dragged his arm over a shoulder. 'Come on. I dare say your guts are in an agony now.'

Strangely, it was his matter-of-fact tone that settled it for Galen. He sagged against Alcuin and allowed him to take the additional weight as they made their erratic way to Brother Benesing's house.

'How is he?' Alcuin asked, as Benesing emerged from seeing to his nephew. He'd waited outside this time and had been growing more impatient by the minute. He'd already paced the garden path a dozen times, and even the burgeoning seedlings and the flowering perennial herbs, buzzing with bees, could offer no distraction.

'I've given him a sleeping draught. He won't wake again until tomorrow. By then we'll also know if there has been any internal damage. You say he fell out of his desk?'

It seemed to Alcuin that Brother Benesing didn't know what to make of what had happened. Alcuin didn't like to see that, especially not from a family member.

'There was a struggle,' Alcuin said, wishing Brother Benesing, of all people, would understand.

'It isn't like Galen to get into a fight,' Benesing said, with a puzzled frown.

'It was forced upon him,' Alcuin said. Seeing Benesing's expression grow all the more troubled, he sighed and added, 'Galen once told me a catamite approached him in this abbey because he thought–'

'Yes,' Benesing said dryly.

'I believe that same catamite tried to force his attentions on Galen again and he resisted.'

'I see,' Benesing said, with a heavy scowl. 'Do you really believe that's what happened?'

'I have the evidence of my own eyes.'

Benesing nodded, but he looked far from convinced.

'Good Lord, why do you doubt him so?' Alcuin said, throwing up his hands.

'I don't know,' Benesing said, and sat down on his garden bench with a heavy sigh. 'Perhaps because he was ever such a gentle boy. He was more like a girl than a boy. It makes it an easier thing to believe of him.'

'I see,' Alcuin said, and he did understand. 'Did Galen resist the last time?'

'Oh yes. Judging by his injuries, he fought like the devil. There was a fragment of human skin lodged between his front teeth, and his hands and arms were badly scratched and bruised. He fought so hard that he broke two fingers, and the nail of the little finger of his right hand was ripped clean out. His face was smashed in and he had bruises all over.

'It's a miracle he survived, actually, because he had a fearsome bruise around his throat where his life had nearly been crushed out of him. When he arrived here, his face was blue and he could barely breathe. I had to cut a slit in his throat and insert a pen so he could get sufficient air.'

'He was lucky you knew that trick,' Alcuin said, and stopped his restless pacing. He hadn't realised quite how hard Galen had fought. Then again, he should have, for he'd seen Galen's desperate resistance today.

'Who else saw this fight?' Benesing asked, looking up at Alcuin and squinting against the sun.

'Everyone who works in the scriptorium and... the abbot came in just as we separated them.'

'I see,' Benesing said. 'What did he say?'

'He ordered them both to be treated and said he'd question them later.'

'Did he give any hint as to whom he believed in this mess?'

'Not one. Waerelm was shouting that he was the injured party. Galen said he did nothing.'

'What else could he say? Who would believe him, though?'

'I would. I will tell the truth of what I saw.'

Alcuin's words seemed to have no effect on Brother Benesing, as the same troubled frown still creased his forehead. Alcuin shook his head. At the very least, family loyalty should have had Brother Benesing pretending to believe in his nephew. Things had come to a desperate pass if even his uncle couldn't feign belief in Galen's innocence. This with a witness standing before him telling him it was a slander.

Chapter 12

G alen was trying his best to keep working while he recovered. His uncle had fetched a gathering and the codex he was copying from, and now he was sitting at his uncle's table in the middle of his hut. The pile of pens, penknife and two sealable ink pots fought for space amongst Benesing's work tools, bundles of herbs and jars of ointment. Possibly because he was taking up too much space, or because his uncle preferred his own company, Benesing had added a small table to his outside bench.

He was now sitting at the door, energetically pounding away with a stone pestle and mortar. He was putting so much energy into this process that his entire right shoulder lifted with each press and added its strength to the grinding.

Galen wished he could give his writing the same amount of effort. It was difficult. He'd thought of the abbey as a sanctuary. In here, he was supposed to be safe. A tremor shook his hand, overtook his entire body and shut down his mind. It kept happening, breaking into his thoughts and disrupting his ability to work.

Galen put down his pen, screwed shut his ink pot, crawled into his bed and pulled the blanket up all the way over his head. He shut his eyes tight, trying to block out the moment Waerelm's lips had pushed against his and how the monk had grabbed at his robes with such determination.

The squeak of the garden gate sent a dart of fear through Galen. Was this the abbot? Galen was living in daily dread of the abbot coming to see him. This time he was convinced he'd be excommunicated and thrown out at best, or put on trial and executed for sodomy at worst.

'Good morning Benesing, is your nephew ready to see me?' came the abbot's voice from outside.

Silence fell as Benesing stopped his grinding. 'You're speaking to him first?'

'Waerelm's injuries, as you know, have become infested with evil spirits. He's feverish and alternates between raving and catatonia.'

This came as news to Galen. His uncle had not told him what had happened to Waerelm, and he'd not asked for fear of where that conversation might lead.

'Aye, I'm aware,' Benesing said. 'That's why I'm making this poultice. It's for his wounds. It will draw the evil humours out.'

'It seems to me his fretting and roaring have more to do with an ailment of the spirit than to the wounds of his arm.'

'He is very unquiet.'

Galen was struck by how neutral his uncle sounded. He was being as careful as he could be not to show allegiance. Galen supposed he couldn't blame him. But tears pricked his eyes to be so distrusted.

'And you have no opinion why he might be in such a state?' Abbot Dyrewine said.

'Would you believe me, when the other person involved in this mess is a member of my family?'

'You are prudent, Benesing, it does you honour.'

The abbot was right, Galen thought, his uncle had even gone so far as to check his penknife surreptitiously one evening.

'You don't suspect your nephew of poisoning Waerelm, do you?' Dyrewine said.

'You must think I believe Galen capable of anything but, I promise you, I don't. I was just worried about what extremes he may have gone to, to protect himself. He surely believed nobody else would lift a finger for him.'

'That seems to be the case, however. After the incident in the scriptorium, Alcuin came to my office, filled with an urgent need to tell me I was being unjust.'

'That is surprising. I thought Alcuin had gone the way of all the other brothers and dropped Galen. And Alcuin hasn't come to my house again after bringing Galen here.'

Galen was as surprised as his uncle to hear of what Alcuin had done. It made him feel better, which was such a strange reaction. He pushed the blanket down so he could hear, but kept his eyes shut tight. A stupid and pointless reflex from childhood where he'd believed if he couldn't see anything, he couldn't be hurt by it.

'Still, I will wait to see what comes of the matter,' the abbot was saying.

'Only if you get to talk to Waerelm, and I fear for his sanity as well as his health these days.'

'As you say, his sanity is at risk.'

'He is a man with a weight on his mind. It made him impossible to control in his rages, and it weighs him down in his stupor. It keeps him from making a recovery.'

'But he must make a recovery, Benesing, I rely on you. This limbo can't continue.'

Galen prayed that Waerelm would make a recovery too. It shocked him to hear how much damage he'd caused. It filled him with regret.

'In the meantime, perhaps Galen should move to a cell,' Benesing said.

Galen wished he hadn't heard that either. It was never good to listen in; it told you more than was good for you. He knew he was a burden on his uncle, and this confirmed it.

'Does he get under your feet?'

Benesing sighed so loudly even Galen could hear it as he said, 'Not really. He's been writing away, copying into the manuscript he and Brother Alcuin are working on. It's just that he's miserable, and I can do without his misery seeping into me whenever I look at him.'

'Very well, I'll have a cell prepared for him. He can work there. I suppose it gives us the advantage that if we lock him in, he will be safe from any further attempts on his body.'

'Why him?' Benesing blurted out, echoing Galen's own perpetual question. 'Why does he attract this attention?'

'Because people have drawn an incorrect conclusion about him. It leaves them to assume he is safe to approach. Perhaps his desperate defence of his person against Brother Waerelm will convince them it would be best not to make the attempt.'

'What is happening, Dyrewine? How many of these

creatures are out there? How can this perversion have spread so far?'

The abbot was silent for a long while as he considered the question, and Galen held his breath, waiting to hear the answer too.

'It has been my observation over the decades I have been an abbot, that our calling provides an almost ideal refuge for catamites. For those who struggle against these unnatural urges, it gives them room to pray and resist. For others it is a place where they can work to ensnare novices and draw them into their web. I have worked hard to discourage that in my abbey, but I am aware, as you must be too, that it happens.'

'I am aware,' Benesing said dryly, much to Galen's surprise. 'How could I not be, as the infirmarius?'

'Indeed.'

'And in defence of my nephew, if he is a sodomite it is my belief that he is of the former type you described, the one who is trying to overcome an unnatural urge.'

'Indeed?' Dyrewine said neutrally. 'Well I'd best speak to him about that directly.'

'He's inside. I ordered him not to leave.'

'You did the right thing,' the abbot said, and Galen realised he'd stepped into the hut.

Now what did he do? Did he keep his eyes screwed shut? No, that was foolish. It took a great deal of effort, but he forced his eyes open and watched the abbot settle on the low stool beside his bed. Galen realised he was holding his breath and took a quick gasp of air.

The abbot gave him a slight smile that Galen found impossible to read.

'Father Abbot,' he said, then, realising he should get up, pushed his blanket aside.

'No, stay where you are.'

Dyrewine placed a firm hand on Galen's shoulder and pushed him back into his pillows.

Galen froze, uncertain of what to do, then subsided back down. He desperately wanted to ask what happened next, but fear always robbed him of his ability to speak.

'I came to hear your side of the story,' Abbot Dyrewine said, shifting on the stool.

It was a bit too low to be comfortable, and Galen wondered why he'd not chosen the chair from the table.

'Start at the beginning and leave nothing out.'

Galen's eyes dropped to the floor. It was easier to concentrate if he wasn't looking straight at the abbot's piercing gaze. He struggled with his thoughts for a moment, to get them in order, and he wrapped his arms tightly around his body, trying to get the shaking under control as he spoke. Then he started in a soft, hesitant voice, laying out one event after the next.

'I'm sorry I stabbed him,' Galen finished. 'Alcuin was already there. I had no more need to fear, but I couldn't stop myself.'

'I see,' the abbot said, and nodded thoughtfully as he gazed down at the floor.

Galen couldn't hold back any longer. One question above all others had bothered him since coming to the abbey. Now was probably his last chance to get his answer.

So Galen gathered up all his courage and said, 'Sodomy is a mortal sin... punishable by death. If... if you believed me guilty of it, why was I not executed?'

'Ah, you have wondered about that, have you?' Dyrewine said, and he rocked back and forth on the stool, apparently giving the question consideration.

'Everyone believes I'm a sodomite. There could be no reason for you to protect me,' Galen said, wondering how foolish this question was. Might it push the abbot into deciding they should execute him after all?

'I don't believe that you are a sodomite.'

Galen's eyes flew up to Dyrewine's face, wide in surprise. 'You... you don't?'

'I may seem like a remote and uncaring man, Galen, but I know very well what is happening in my abbey. I interrogated your uncle on your character and the nature of your injuries, when you arrived. I also had a lengthy conversation with your confessor once you were well enough to make your confession to him.'

Galen felt sick upon hearing this and said, 'The confessional is supposed to be sacred.'

'I didn't ask him to break that sanctity. I merely asked him whether you were a sodomite. He gave it as his opinion that you are not.'

A tear slipped from Galen's eye, and he gave a quick nod. Even after his father had disowned him and the rest of the abbey treated him as a pariah, the abbot didn't think he was a catamite? At least that explained one mystery that had bothered Galen so much.

'I should probably have told you all of this before, but I'm afraid I'm not a very emotional man,' the abbot said, 'so speaking of such things doesn't come easily to me. I have watched you, Galen, from the day you first arrived at the abbey. In that time I came to realise that you are a soul in torment. For a man like me... you seem to feel far too much. More than is good for you. And because I can't understand it, I can't really help you.'

'I'm sorry,' Galen whispered, ashamed in the same way before the abbot as he always felt when he'd stood before his father.

'There is no need to apologise,' the abbot said. 'I just wish... If you could only hold your head up, look people in the eye and dare them to cast aspersions on you, you might already be on the path to becoming a member of the community.'

'I can't,' Galen said, and even now he couldn't look the abbot full in the face. It wasn't in his nature to be able to do that. His shyness, coupled with the constant pain he endured, took from him this one way out of his predicament.

'It might interest you to know,' the abbot continued, 'that I have sustained an impassioned meeting with Alcuin, urging me to consider your unenviable position that makes suspicion fall upon you automatically. He told me several other revealing things. Words you had spoken, actions of Waerelm's. It made Alcuin doubt his friend. And mind you, I am telling you that Alcuin stood before me, no doubt quaking in his shoes, to tell me that his friend Waerelm was the sodomite. He was clear that it is not you, the outcast of my community, as everyone else believed.'

'He did?' Galen said, glad of the additional detail, even if he'd already heard the gist of it in the abbot's earlier conversation with his uncle.

A flicker of hope touched Galen's heart. He realised that it was more because of Alcuin's actions than that the abbot might believe his side of the tale. How odd, when it was the abbot who held his life in his hands.

'I will speak to Waerelm next. He is feverish this morning, so my interrogation will have to wait.'

'All he did was kiss me, but... I stabbed him,' Galen said, and couldn't suppress a shudder as he spoke.

'I like your sense of justice,' the abbot said. 'Someone who suffered as horrific a rape as you, who flinches now at any touch, has emphasised the relative triviality of what happened. But who knows what might have happened next if the other brothers hadn't arrived? And who knows what Waerelm might have tried, days and weeks afterwards, if his first clumsy attempts had been successful.'

Galen nodded. The abbot had put his finger precisely on what he had feared. That was why he'd not been able to stop himself.

'You should rest,' Dyrewine said. 'Stay in this house as your uncle ordered until I come back to you. And rest assured, it is I, and no-one else, who will bring you my verdict.'

Chapter 13

While the abbey waited for Waerelm to pull through his fever, Alcuin was struggling under a new and unaccustomed sensation. He was a handsome man; in his youth he'd been a charming boy and much admired. He could easily have become a warrior, a thane in his father's entourage. But at an early age people had marvelled over his artistic ability. As the youngest son, it was therefore decided that he would become a monk and an illuminator. His entry into the brotherhood had been one of honour and eager expectation. From the day he'd arrived as a novice, he had been feted and cosseted.

But here he'd transgressed an unspoken rule. He'd not kept a proper distance from an outcast. His first attempts had brought direct censure. His second defence of Galen had resulted in no open words against him. How could they, when so many people had been a witness to what had happened? But he was suffering from a distinct freezing of relations. There was a chilling towards him he'd never had to deal with in his privileged life.

It was a chastening experience, and not one he relished. He stayed away from Galen partly because of it, but also because Galen had pushed him away. He'd been unwilling to accept for a second time that Alcuin meant him any friendship. Who could blame Galen when he'd been such a coward before? Why trust a man when he buckled so easily under the mildest of disapproval?

Alcuin felt puzzled by his own lack of character; ashamed that he'd so easily succumbed to the majority view. He scarcely recognised that behaviour in the image he had of himself as a good and righteous man. True, he'd salvaged some of it for himself when he'd gone to see the abbot to speak up for Galen. Even though he was disappointed, if not surprised, when nobody else had said a word about the incident. But it left him feeling ashamed and less moved by this very mild ostracism he was now experiencing.

It was nothing to what Galen suffered. Alcuin kept his bed in the dormitory's corner, his desk remained on the dais, and his friends sat beside him in the refectory. But their conversation was guarded. Their laughter was too ready to spring to their lips, and too loud, as if to hide discomfort, and they cast their eyes about, watching those around them. They were hoping they weren't being judged unfavourably for remaining as Alcuin's friends. How he was coming to hate this hypocrisy. How he prayed for Waerelm to recover soon so that the abbot could pronounce his judgement and they could all go back to their old ways.

Well, perhaps not all their old ways. Alcuin was doggedly determined that this time he wouldn't let Galen down. This time he would talk to him whenever he wished. He would walk with him and sometimes even sit beside him in the refectory, no matter what kinds of things they said to him about it afterwards.

But not yet. For the moment he had to be patient and just get on with his work, as Galen was doing, locked up in a cell all on his own. Alcuin couldn't understand why. But as nobody had been officially informed of the reason, most of the conjecture was that it was a tacit acceptance of Galen's guilt. Alcuin couldn't bring himself to be optimistic that the abbot had taken the least heed of anything he'd said.

It was with considerable surprise, therefore, that one morning, as Alcuin and his brothers were making their way to the church, they noticed a small group of monks, the abbot amongst them, standing at the gate of the abbey with Waerelm. He didn't look well. He seemed unnaturally pale and was propping himself up against a staff.

'Look at that,' Brother Anfred murmured. 'They're sending him off.'

'Why would they do that?' Alcuin said. 'He isn't even wearing his habit.'

'No,' Anfred said, and his eyes narrowed thoughtfully.

'What are you thinking?'

'That we will soon see Galen back in our midst.'

'Really?'

Anfred shrugged and said, 'I saw what you saw in the scriptorium. We all did. And honestly, Galen attacking Waerelm? Galen is by far the smaller man, and timid to boot. No, impossible. I also noticed how over-the-top Waerelm was in his hatred of Galen whenever he spoke of him. Sometimes I even wondered about it.'

'You suspected Waerelm?'

Anfred smiled grimly and said, 'My mistake was that I thought he'd conceived a passion for you, not for little Galen. It seems I was mistaken.'

'And yet you shun Galen?' Alcuin said in shocked amazement and growing anger.

'What do I know of him?'

'What have you ever tried to know?' Alcuin said bitterly.

Anfred smiled knowingly at Alcuin and said, 'You are still young, you'll learn soon enough that it is best to mind your own business.'

'Is that what everyone is trying to let me know now with their coldness?'

'It is a hard lesson for you, isn't it?'

'And I must be a stubborn student, for I seem to draw the wrong conclusions,' Alcuin said. 'I won't distance myself from Galen. Not for such a minor reason as I am given now!'

'Do as you please, Alcuin. But don't be surprised if you find yourself an outcast too,' Anfred said as they passed into the church and the conversation had to cease.

The abbot confirmed Alcuin and Anfred's conjecture at the chapter meeting. He announced, briefly and without fanfare, that he'd interrogated both Waerelm and Galen. Waerelm had finally admitted that Galen was the entirely innocent victim of his attempts to force himself onto the young scribe.

'It won't make him more welcome in our midst though,' Anfred murmured.

And Alcuin knew he was right. Far too many people suspected Galen. Just because they had proved him innocent of this incident, voices were still likely to whisper that he drew that kind of attention because of his reputation. He would remain an outcast.

Chapter 14

A blustery spring turned into a mild summer. With it came a change to the pace and length of their days at the abbey that Galen liked. At times it had felt like his tumultuous winter would never end. His period of confinement in the cells had been a mixture of comfort and deep loneliness.

In the cell he was free from the whispers and suspicious glances of his peers. He also didn't move much. He could work seated on his small cot, with the table drawn up to it. It was far more comfortable than his usual writing desk.

The problem was, the cell didn't provide as much light as the scriptorium. Galen often found himself hunched too close to the page as he struggled to see what he was doing. It strained his eyes and his back.

It was also very quiet. The abbey's cells were at some distance from the rest of the buildings. Galen supposed it was to keep those who had committed a crime from spreading their evil. The only time Galen saw anybody was when one of the lay brothers, who worked as a servant at the abbey, came to bring him his meal. A second man would arrive each morning to empty his chamber pot.

Although the abbot had told him he was being locked away for his own safety, the lay brothers didn't seem to be aware of it. They never said a word to him. Conversation between the monks and the lay brothers wasn't encouraged, but a smile and a greeting would have been nice.

Despite his shyness, Galen liked people. When he lived at home there was nothing he enjoyed more than sitting in the sewing room with his mother and his sisters as they gossiped. It was a little more difficult for him in his father's hall. He struggled to put himself forward. But he liked to sit, unnoticed, near the fire, listening to all the shared tales, jokes and riddles.

Even at the abbey, he had the chapter meetings and the banter of the scriptorium. At the very least, he had human company. So, despite the discomfort, it relieved Galen when he was given permission to leave the cells.

He slipped into the scriptorium after Terce, with the book and his work implements in a sling bag. He laid them out at his desk before sitting down. The armarius ignored him, as did everyone else.

But Galen noticed that Alcuin smiled to see him back, even though he didn't raise his head from his work. That, combined with the bright, warm, summer sunshine streaming in through the window, made Galen's day. Although writing all day was gruelling, Galen enjoyed it. It gave him something to occupy his time and his mind. Today, though, he set to work with unaccustomed enthusiasm.

Just before they all packed up for Sext and dinner, Alcuin

tucked a gathering under his arm and slipped from his desk. Galen waited for him to come over. Alcuin was smiling and, although Galen didn't smile back, he hoped Alcuin knew that he was welcome.

'May I have a look?'

Galen gave a quick nod and said softly, 'This chapter is all about how a pair of crows was stealing the thatch from Cuthbert's monastery, so he admonished them not to do so or he would banish them. They ignored him, so he cast them out. Then one of the pair returned and abased itself on the ground, its wings spread out in supplication. Cuthbert, in his mercy, forgave it and allowed the pair to return to the monastery. So in thanks, the crow brought him a lump of lard with which to grease the monks' shoes.'

'What a strange story,' Alcuin said. 'Although it will be fun to draw a pair of crows.'

'It's intended to show that man can learn from the animals. They were not too proud to beg for forgiveness.'

Galen had already learned that Alcuin's thoughts were always about the images he might draw, and not the lessons to be learned from each tale. He supposed that was how it should be for an illuminator.

'Here,' Alcuin said, handing over the gathering he'd been holding. 'I thought you might like to see it. It's what you were working on when Waerelm... well, you know. As you can see, I painted over most of the spilled ink and blood. It did no harm. I worked the remaining stains into illustrations and marginalia. It helps that the chapter was all about a fire the devil set and that Cuthbert put out by prayer. I could hide most of the damage in the images of flames. In the end it will be a very fine codex, never fear.'

Galen was deeply relieved to see that accident hadn't harmed the book or resulted in him having to rewrite anything. It was also a pleasure to see more of Alcuin's fine work. He looked up from examining the gathering and gave a hesitant, accepting nod, his eyes searching Alcuin's face.

'The abbot is also very pleased with the work,' Alcuin said, surprising Galen by extending the conversation beyond what they normally had. 'He's also decided on what our next project should be.'

'He has?' Galen said, now doubly surprised. Apparently, neither the abbot nor Alcuin had any hesitation about using him as the scribe for yet another book.

'Between you and me,' Alcuin said, leaning in conspiratorially and dropping his voice to a whisper, 'I think he's worried about the approaching millennium. He wants something magnificent in readiness for the second coming.'

Galen knew that he was gaping in astonishment. Partly it was because of the abbot's fears. Mainly it was because this was the closest he'd come to gossip in his three years at the abbey.

Alcuin winked and might have said more, but Brother Haenric shouted across the room, 'Come on, Alcuin, it's time for dinner and I'm starving.'

'Greedy sod,' Alcuin said. 'It's only midday. I haven't adjusted to the summer timetable or the earlier meal yet and he's already howling that he's hungry.'

Galen hadn't a clue what to say about that. The discomfort he always felt in his nether regions left him with very little appetite at the best of times.

'Do you need some help to get down from the desk?' Alcuin said, further surprising Galen.

'No!' he said hastily, and then flushed. 'I can do it.'

'So you are recovered from your mauling?'

Galen gave a quick nod.

'Fine, well, I'll see you later,' Alcuin said, and headed off after Brothers Anfred, Haenric and Toffa.

Galen wondered what Alcuin's reception would be like in that little group after he'd spent so much time chatting with him. In the event, they just separated to allow him in. Galen watched as he followed slowly after them, and still there was nothing. He'd seen Alcuin being scolded before for paying him the mild attention he had. He wondered what had changed.

Over the next couple of days, Alcuin made it a habit to look at Galen's work just before they headed to dinner. On the alternating days, when they shared a plate of supplementary food, Alcuin also made a point of sitting beside Galen and ensuring he got exactly half of what was on the plate. Galen wondered what Brother Tostig made of this. Whatever it was, he was apparently too wary of Alcuin to make a fuss. And still Alcuin's friends said nothing.

Galen knew that curiosity was his abiding sin and should be resisted, but this mystery had to be explained. So, one day, when Alcuin came for his usual progress inspection, Galen asked the question that had been distracting him for days.

He lowered his voice so that the others wouldn't hear, and murmured, 'Why aren't your friends giving you a hard time about me anymore?'

Alcuin laughed at the question before saying, 'I suppose

they don't feel they have the right.'

'They don't? Why not?' Galen asked, because the answer made no sense.

'It turns out that they already knew what Waerelm was. Or at the very least, they suspected. But they remained his friend, despite that knowledge. They said nothing when he attacked you, even though they all saw exactly what I saw. So how can they berate me now for merely talking to you?'

'I see,' Galen said, and looked around the scriptorium at the other brothers who were heads down, engaged in their work. There was a time when they'd all have paused to hear what Alcuin and Galen were saying. 'They knew about Waerelm?'

'I suppose he was the one you mentioned before, that...' Alcuin tailed off with a meaningful look and wiggle of his head.

'He was.'

Galen felt like he should have been angry at the other monks for shunning him when they left Waerelm alone. But he felt no rage. He understood why he had been treated differently.

He'd arrived at the abbey as a stranger with a black sin to his name. They'd grown up with Waerelm. They probably only gradually started to suspect him. By which time they were willing to let it slide. Presumably, he'd never approached one of them the way he'd approached Galen.

So that was one mystery explained. Galen felt better knowing it. He was relieved that Alcuin wouldn't suffer through their association.

As the summer progressed, Galen came to look upon their

daily meeting as a commonplace. He was glad they were no longer marred by the fear of what the other monks would say to Alcuin. That, combined with their book nearing completion, made it the best season Galen had spent in Yarmwick so far. He prayed that, as life had improved, it would continue to get better.

Chapter 15

Summer slipped gently into a misty autumn. It was at this time that Alcuin felt the impact of the nearby marshes most intensely. He'd never experienced quite so much mist and fog in his life. It made him miserable. It was as if the humidity wrapped itself around him and the cold slipped deep into his bones.

At this point he was looking forward to the winter. He preferred crisp and cold-but-bright days to this blanketing fog. The dimmer days also made it difficult to work. They could use candles, but the flickering light wasn't helpful when he was trying to produce his detailed work.

Whenever he could, therefore, Alcuin huddled in the warming room. It was a blessed respite from the cold of the rest of the abbey. If he had anything to say against life as a monk, it would be a complaint about the perpetual cold they endured. It was at times like this that Alcuin most missed the roaring fire of his father's great hall.

The warming room itself was a quarter of the size of the refectory. It had a low ceiling that was blackened by the smoke which rose from the fireplace that dominated one wall. A fire, large enough to rival any an ealdorman might provide, burned merrily in that wide space and stone benches stood to either side. They were the most sought-after on a day like this, as they were closest to the blaze and so also warmed by the fire. The high-backed benches that ringed the rest of the room were wooden and identical to the pews in the church. Alcuin settled himself in one of these, as they prevented a draught from whistling round his back. He'd noticed, when he'd arrived nearly a year ago now, that the wall on this side of the room was also warm because the fireplace for the kitchen was next door.

There was always a sense of camaraderie in the warming room which attracted Alcuin to it for more than just its physical warmth. In this room the hierarchy of the abbey broke down, and man could talk to man like the brothers they called themselves.

His only regret was that Galen seldom came to the warming room. When he did, he sat back in the shadows, his hood pulled down low to hide his face. He never attempted to join in with the rest of the monks' conversation. Alcuin had once tried to draw him into conversation here, in front of everyone, and Galen had withdrawn so quickly that he knew better than to make a second attempt.

So when Galen slipped inside and settled in a quiet corner of the room, Alcuin did no more than cast him a friendly smile before going back to the deep theological debate he was having with Brother Anfred and Brother Haward, the chamberlain, on the effect the coming millennium would have.

Brother Anfred was of the opinion that the antichrist's arrival was imminent.

'The signs are everywhere. I heard tell that dragons have been seen flying over the kingdom of York.'

'Yes,' Brother Haenric agreed, 'and in Mercia a giant destroyed all the villages along the River Dee.'

'Where do you hear such things?' Alcuin said with a laugh.

'It isn't funny, Brother Alcuin,' Haenric muttered. 'The lay brothers get their news from the town when they are fetching supplies.'

'And you believe them?'

'Why wouldn't we?'

'Because they are uneducated illiterates,' Alcuin said, and glanced in Galen's direction. All he could see of Galen's face under his hood was his mouth, but that was smiling.

'You shouldn't discount the signs that are all around us,' Brother Anfred said, 'for they are a warning.'

'I know, of the antichrist,' Alcuin said.

'Exactly. He must precede the arrival of Christ, you know.'

As if on cue, the sound of a horn heralding visitors at the foregate interrupted their conversation.

'In this weather?' Anfred murmured, and went to join the huddle of monks at the window that looked out onto the cemetery and the main gate to the abbey.

Alcuin pushed eagerly through the crowd of men to get a better view. Visitors were always welcome and frequently produced an outpouring of images for his illustrations. He liked new things and the stranger they were, the better. He was in time to see a group of nobles ride into the courtyard, their horses making eddies in the mist. A group of lay brothers, along with Brother Kenric, ran out to help them down from their horses.

A powerfully built middle-aged man jumped from his horse unaided, pushed back his hood to reveal a shock of greying brown hair, and took an unsmiling look around. The grimness of his expression struck Alcuin. It also pricked his interest. He looked like the leader of this band. He was armed and richly dressed, so he had to be a noble.

His companions looked like thanes and as tough a bunch of men as Alcuin had ever laid eyes on. This was especially true of the red-headed giant who dismounted and joined the leader. They exchanged a few desultory words. Even from Alcuin's distance, it felt like there was tension between the two of them. Now what were they doing here?

'Galen,' Brother Benesing said hollowly, 'it's your father.'

Benesing's words hit Galen like a heavy stone. He was stunned, unable to think, unable to move. The room spun about him and, out of that haze, Alcuin's face appeared.

He grasped Galen firmly by the elbow, which thankfully helped keep him upright.

'Galen, are you alright?'

Galen stared blankly at Alcuin. The terror that always lurked at the back of his mind had taken over. He didn't know what to do.

'Help me!' Galen whispered.

'Of course, anything. What do you want me to do?'

'Is he alone?' Galen doubted it, but it was the most important question.

'No, he's brought a band of thanes with him.'

So this was it - what he had dreaded had come to pass.

'I have to get away,' Galen said, fighting the rising panic as he took a jerky step towards the door.

'Where to?'

'Anywhere. He mustn't find me,' Galen said, and he broke into a run. He hadn't run in years. It tore at his insides but he didn't care.

Alcuin ran after Galen and caught up with him when he was halfway down the cloister.

'Galen, slow down,' Alcuin said and grabbed onto his robe. 'You'll do yourself an injury.'

Galen couldn't do that. He staggered on, tears of terror running down his face. 'I have to get away. I have to get away!' he muttered, and his hands pushed ineffectually against Alcuin's restraining grasp.

'Well, there's no escape from the abbey. Those thanes with your father are bound to be watching the gate.'

'Then I must hide!'

'Why?'

'Because he'll kill me!' Galen shouted.

Alcuin jerked back in surprise.

'The church,' he said. 'You can hide in the church. They won't find you there and even if they do, they can't harm you on consecrated ground.'

Galen shuddered and shook his head. He doubted that was true. But he allowed himself to be hurried along the corridor, out of a side door and then, keeping on the lookout against anyone who might see them, they slipped into the church.

To Galen's surprise, Alcuin made for the Lady Chapel. It

was as if divine inspiration had guided him to take Galen to the place he'd feel safest.

'There are dozens of hiding places in here. They could search for ages and not find you in the church.'

Galen gave a grunt of pain as his legs caved and he sagged to the floor.

'You shouldn't have tried to run. Have you injured yourself again?' Alcuin said, looking more alarmed by Galen's pallor and his high, fast breath than about the need to hide him.

'It doesn't matter,' Galen gasped.

'Alright, I suppose it doesn't matter right now. Here, hide under this altar,' Alcuin said, as he flipped up the heavily embroidered altar cloth and dragged Galen across the floor and under the thick, oak table. Galen gasped as the pain tore at his insides, and curled himself into a ball.

'I have to go,' Alcuin said. 'Everyone saw me leaving the warming room with you. The abbot is bound to question me.' He must have seen the flicker of fear in Galen's eyes because he said, 'Don't worry, I know how to keep my mouth shut. I'll try to bring you some food later, but if I'm watched, I won't come. Do you understand?'

Galen nodded; he was so racked with terror that he couldn't speak. Alcuin was apparently satisfied though, because he replaced the altar cloth and hurried from the church. Galen wrapped his fist tightly around a corner of the altar cloth as if it were a talisman. As if his mother were there to protect him and interpose her body between him and any danger, as she had always tried to do for him. At the same time, he sent up desperate prayers to God to keep him safe.

Footsteps sounded in the church that sent another bolt of

fear through Galen. It intensified as the voice of the abbot said, 'What can I do for you, Ealdorman Hugh?'

No! How could it be? Did they already know where he was? Had Alcuin betrayed him? Surely not. It was more likely he'd been spotted coming out of the church.

With a trembling hand, Galen slipped his penknife out of his sleeve. He was supposed to leave it in the scriptorium, but he'd taken to always keeping it with him, just in case. If he was going to be dragged away, he would at least put up a fight.

'It has been a while since we were last together, has it not?' the abbot said, as he made his way further up the nave of the church, towards the choir.

'Has it?' the ealdorman said. 'I'm afraid I don't recall.'

Galen put his eye to the gap he'd made when he grabbed the altar cloth. Through it he could see his father. Aside from greyer hair, he looked unchanged. He was still a powerfully built man with broad shoulders and the same hard, uncompromising eyes that had always left Galen tongue-tied in his presence.

'We were both paying attendance to the king in Thetford. I'm not surprised you don't remember me.' The abbot spoke gently, but any of his monks would know he was chiding the ealdorman for his rudeness. 'Now, what can I and my humble abbey do for you today?'

'I've come to see Galen of–' Hugh stopped abruptly and snapped, 'What does he call himself these days?'

'Just Brother Galen, nothing more,' Dyrewine said, as he settled on the front row of the choir and indicated for Hugh to take the row opposite. It kept several broad paces between the men.

Galen knew full well that wouldn't protect the abbot if his father meant him harm, even when it looked like he'd left his weapons outside.

'Typical!' Hugh said, making no move to sit down. 'He makes himself out to be a nobody!'

'He couldn't continue to use your name; you disowned him,' the abbot said, and to Galen's ears he sounded remarkably calm. He wished he had that ability.

'And you let him in,' Hugh said, standing, his legs spread apart, his hands on his hips, like a man giving a severe scolding.

'He wasn't mine to disown,' Dyrewine said.

'You know that isn't what I meant,' Hugh said. 'You took him in when sodomy is a mortal sin and a capital crime.'

'Murder is a mortal sin and a capital crime too, but I am not aware that we condemn the victim for it.'

'A moot point when the victim is dead.'

'You should understand my reasoning, nevertheless.'

'Are you saying that Galen was an innocent victim?'

'I believe so.'

'He could have resisted. He could have prevented it,' Hugh said, and finally sat down.

He sprawled in the choir seat in a way that would have earned any monk a rebuke if they'd tried it in front of their abbot.

It was a painful discussion to hear, and part of Galen wished he wasn't present. But another part knew that it was vital that he understood why, after all these years, his father had come. He wasn't a vain man; he hadn't believed the visit was about him. He'd just feared what might happen if his father did come to the abbey, whatever his reason.

'My analogy with a murder victim stands,' Abbot Dyrewine said. 'They oft resist fiercely, and still they die. I saw Galen's injuries when he arrived. I doubt any man could have fought more strenuously than he did, but a superior force clearly overwhelmed him.'

'He brought it upon himself. He was always more like a girl than a man. He's too soft by half.'

'He is what God made him. He wasn't given the body of a warrior, but God gave him a talent. He is the best scribe I have.'

'I have no use for scribes!'

'No, so I have heard tell.'

'What does that mean?' Hugh said, and an angry light flared in his eyes. It made Galen squirm to see it again. He had oft provoked that same angry glare in his father.

'You are famous throughout the land, Ealdorman Hugh, as an awesome warrior and for being fierce in your loyalty to the men you admire. They are all strong men, like the king, and the thanes you surround yourself with.'

'And you think none of them has the brains to suffice an ant,' Hugh said with an amused smile.

That made the abbot pause and examine Hugh again. This was what most people didn't know about his father, Galen thought. He wasn't just strong and overwhelming in his forceful personality. He was clever too. Here he was displaying his intelligence. He'd come in using blustering, bullyboy tactics designed to overawe the weak of spirit, because it was the quickest and easiest thing to do. That had failed, so now he'd changed tack. He'd switched to a frightening charm. Galen knew full well that it was equally, or possibly even more, dangerous.

'Maybe Galen gets his brains from you after all,' Dyrewine murmured.

'His mother is every bit as clever as I am,' Hugh said. 'Now where is he? I want to see him.'

'Why?'

'Do I not have that right?'

'You disowned him. You have no rights over him.'

Galen was surprised to see that the abbot had discomforted his father, as Hugh shifted uneasily in his chair.

'I have good reason why I must, and will, see Galen.'

'Then you will have to share it with me.'

'No.'

Dyrewine gave him a humourless smile and said, 'Without my help you will never find him in this place.'

'He didn't know I was coming. He won't have had time to hide.'

'On the contrary, I have been informed that he has already hidden.'

'Then I will turn the abbey upside down until I find him.'

Galen stifled a gasp. His father would do exactly what he said he would, but what had precipitated the need for such extreme measures?

'I am almost tempted to let you try,' Dyrewine said, and it looked like he was working hard to control his temper. 'I don't think, however, that I'd like the inconvenience. It would force me to send a strongly worded letter of complaint on the matter to the king and the pope.'

'Damn you, Dyrewine,' Hugh said with a laugh. 'What must I do for you to let me see my s– Galen?'

'Tell me why, after three years, you suddenly have a wish to see him.'

'Huh, I was afraid that was your reason for withholding access.'

'It seems a reasonable request to me.'

'Oh yes, but it forces me to reveal something I'm not at all proud of,' Hugh said, trying to turn off these bitter words with insouciance.

'Perhaps you will feel better for having shared them with me.'

'The cleansing power of the confessional, is it? Well, I've tried that. It didn't work. Very well. I have to see Galen because he wasn't the only one to be attacked.'

'No?'

'It surprises you?'

'Not so much, perhaps. Anyone as depraved as the man who attacked Galen was bound not to stop at one such criminal act.'

The abbot mightn't be surprised, but the news came as a shock to Galen. Before his attack, no such thing had happened in the burh. Then he'd been hustled away and, what with a long and painful recovery and struggling to fit in, Galen had tried to forget the past. It was too painful to dwell on, anyway. It had never occurred to him that what had happened to him might happen again. It made him feel so sick, he was within moments of throwing up.

'He didn't stop,' Hugh said, which pulled Galen's fearful gaze back to him.

He had to learn more, even if it was dreadful.

Hugh ran his hands through his hair in an unfamiliar, rueful gesture and said, 'It shocked me when I came upon Galen's body. I was horrified by what I thought I was seeing, and far too ready to believe that one of my blood might bear that fatal taint. With the kind of boy Galen was, it was all too easy to believe. I thought him a willing party to that depraved act. I thought by washing my hands of him, by removing him from my burh, I had ended the matter.'

'Did you never ask him who the other man was?'

'No,' Hugh said sharply. 'Call me a fool if you like, but I convinced myself that the man responsible was some churl smuggled in by Galen, and I didn't care to find him.'

'What changed your mind?'

'I was forced to face up to the problem when it happened again.'

'When was that?'

'Nothing happened for well over a year after Galen left us. I'd ceased even to think of that episode when one of the people in my burh was killed. His body was left in the same way as Galen's had been, only this one was dead. Strangled. Well, it was in the town and I reasoned that Galen's churl had been involved.'

Dyrewine arched a sceptical eyebrow.

'I know,' Hugh snapped. 'The power of self-deception is great. Anyway, we investigated but found nothing. Then we got another period of quiet. I wasn't happy, though, because now I knew we would have this again. And I wasn't wrong. First one of my thralls was found sodomised and strangled. Finally, a few days ago, it was a thane. They were all done to death in the same way.'

It horrified Galen to hear of the misfortunes that had overcome three more men. The nightmare that woke him sweating and crying in the middle of the night reared up, obliterating his view of the abbot and his father leaning forward, talking to each other across an uncomfortably wide gap.

Galen had great ham-like hands wrapped around his throat, crushing the life out of him as he swung in the air, kicking out, trying to get at the man, scratching at those fingers of iron to pull them free, blood drumming in his ears, his neck so stretched it felt like his head might be torn from his body.

'So now you've finally come to speak to the only witness who is still alive.' The abbot's voice came from far away, drawing Galen back. He put his hand over his mouth to stifle his quick gasps lest they be overheard.

'He must help me,' Hugh said.

'That may be more difficult than you realise. Galen has never spoken to anyone here about the attack, nor mentioned the name of the attacker. I doubt he'll want to speak to you about him either.'

'Well, speak he must, or another will suffer and die.'

'Yes, perhaps that will be sufficient argument to convince him to see you.'

'I don't see the difficulty,' Hugh said. 'Why all this delay?'

'Good Lord, Ealdorman,' Dyrewine said, 'I am considered an unsympathetic and dense man by many of my people, but next to you I look like an over-sensitive maiden.'

'I don't know what you're talking about,' Hugh said. He

jumped up and paced restlessly around the choir before flinging himself back into the chair.

'Do you know what happened to your son once he got here?'

'You told me,' Hugh said, tapping his hand on one knee impatiently. 'He became a scribe.'

'He did, but that is only a part of the story. He arrived here at death's door. It took a long time for him to heal. Something, I'm sorry to say, which has not been entirely successful.'

'He still suffers?'

'His uncle tells me he is in constant pain. I imagine it is a very great pain, for he is always in a stoop and moves very slowly.'

'I see.'

'No, you don't, there is more. It is impossible to keep secrets in a community such as mine. The fact that Galen was sodomised, rapidly became common knowledge. As you've said, it's a sin, and the brothers, like you, decided that Galen was a catamite. They, too, shun him. Barely a soul has spoken to him in the years he has been here. His has been a lonely, ostracised position.'

'He doesn't have the strength of character to bear that,' Hugh said, shaking his head.

'He had no choice, but it has been a struggle. If he didn't have his work, he may well have succumbed.'

Hugh nodded thoughtfully, his eyes fixed on the abbot. Dyrewine watched him back, waiting. Galen held his breath and wondered what he would do. Could he face his father again?

'For all that, you know I must see him,' Hugh said. 'Otherwise you will have another death on your hands, just as I have on mine.'

'Yes,' Dyrewine said. 'We must bring this sodomite of yours to justice. I will find Galen and convince him to speak to you. But don't be surprised if there are conditions.'

'I can accept that, just don't delay too long,' Hugh said.

'Rest assured, I won't,' Dyrewine said. 'I will get my monks to take you to our guest quarters and provide you with food and drink. It is a long way from your burh to here. No doubt you could use some rest. Make sure you and your men remain in the guesthouse. If I see anyone wandering about the abbey, or searching for Galen, I will expel the lot of you.'

The ealdorman gave a slight sardonic laugh at the idea of anyone being able to boot him out of anywhere, but he nodded and said, 'I will do as you wish. Show me these quarters.'

'Go back outside. Brother Kenric will accompany you and your men.'

With a brief nod and a swirl of his cape, Hugh left. The abbot stayed where he was until long after the sound of the men had vanished into the abbey. Then he gave a deep, pensive sigh and said loudly enough that his voice could be heard around the church, 'Galen, are you here?'

Galen gasped. How did the abbot know?

'If I was going to hide, the church would be where I'd come first,' the abbot said. 'Please, if you are here and you heard Ealdorman Hugh, you know you need to speak to him, don't you?'

Galen felt his familiar paralysis of indecision coming over

him, but the abbot was right. He couldn't allow anybody else to die because of his silence.

He pushed the altar cloth aside and whispered, 'I'm here,' although he didn't have the strength to push himself to his feet.

'Ah,' the abbot said, and hurried over. He sat down at the end of the pew, facing Galen. 'Are you alright?'

Galen nodded. He was in a lot of pain and, worse, he was in emotional turmoil.

'Yes, Ealdorman Hugh needs to know,' he said, with difficulty, 'but I fear the rapist will try to silence me before I can say anything.'

'Then we'd best get this done quickly, before he has a chance to find you,' the abbot said. 'Wait here, I will make the necessary arrangements.'

Chapter 16

And so it was, that as dusk fell, Galen found himself sitting on the steps that led from the nave to the chancel, with a group of monks guarding the entrance to the church, clubs at the ready, the abbot at their head. Galen doubted that the motley assemblage of monks could stand against even a single one of his father's men, but his decision was now made. He couldn't have made any other. His fate, one way or another, was about to be decided.

Ealdorman Hugh stepped into the church and paused for a moment on the threshold as his eyes adjusted to the gloom. It was cold, and his breath billowed about him like the fog outside. Then he took a deep breath, blew it out in a long stream, and walked towards the chancel. Each footstep rang out like approaching doom in the silence of the church.

Galen wished he could stand for this encounter, but that was impossible. He'd done himself an injury with his run. Besides, at best he'd be standing stooped over, and that would irritate Ealdorman Hugh. He liked thanes who stood tall and proud, daring anyone to challenge them. Even if Galen were fit and well, his head would bow. He was incapable of meeting Hugh's piercing gaze that measured him and found him wanting.

So Galen sat, a huddle of black cloth, on the steps, lit by the pair of candelabras that stood on the main altar. His left arm was drawn up tight against his body. He'd twisted his right arm up over his head, his hand grasping his shaved scalp, his fingers running over the bristle of his tonsure.

'Galen,' Hugh said.

How had he arrived so quickly? Galen looked up with a gasp, and Hugh took an involuntary step back, which surprised Galen.

'Dear Mother of God,' Hugh muttered. 'You look like a wraith.'

Galen had nothing he could say to that, and, as always, he quailed under Hugh's hard stare. It felt as if it were boring right through him. He couldn't take it, and his gaze dropped to the floor where all he could see were his father's feet.

Hugh stood for a moment, then, with an unexpected sigh, he sat down on the chair they'd brought in for him. The creak of the wood as he settled sounded loud in the church.

'The abbot told me you've been ill. I see he didn't exaggerate.'

'No.' Galen wished that at least his voice could be firm and clear, but even in this he failed.

'Did he tell you why I have come?'

Galen glanced up, surprised. So the abbot hadn't told his father that he'd been in the church all along. 'He did.'

Hugh nodded, and Galen didn't know what to do. As always with his father, he was tongue-tied and terrified, waiting for him to ask his questions. He doubted he'd be believed, which added a deep sense of futility.

Hugh gave an exasperated tut and shifted in his chair, but said nothing. That was unusual. It wasn't like his father to remain silent and to just sit and wait. His impatience was legendary. He should already have been roaring at Galen to stop wasting his time and speak.

'Does... does my mother know you are here?'

Galen surprised himself with the question because it had come out of nowhere. Well, maybe not that. He was desperate for news of his mother and sisters.

'What?' Hugh muttered. Then much to Galen's surprise, instead of getting angry and telling him not to talk rubbish, Hugh said, 'She does.'

'Did she send a message for me?'

'She's unlikely to send anything via me. After I turned my back on you, she stopped speaking to me.'

'Oh,' Galen said, and subsided back into silence. It had been a stupid question, merely delaying the inevitable.

'Your brother Willnoth was killed.'

The news came as such a shock that Galen gave a start. Strong, invincible, brave Willnoth was dead?

'I am sorry,' Galen murmured, filled with sorrow for his father and more for his mother who must be in great pain over the death of her firstborn. 'I know how much you loved him.'

Hugh stiffened at these words, although Galen couldn't understand why they might offend him. Hugh's brow furrowed in anger, then he shook away that flash of temper.

'He died in battle... fighting against the damned invading

Vikings.'

'An honourable way to die,' Galen said, and wondered whether his father was also trying to delay the inevitable.

'Yes,' Hugh said. 'The abbot tells me you're a good scribe.'

Galen shrugged, and his eyes flicked briefly up to his father's face. There was no doubt now that he was putting off the tough conversation that had to come next, for surely he had no interest in whether or not Galen was a good scribe.

Galen feared what Hugh would say and do when they finally did get to the point. The silence between them now felt oppressive. It was only broken by the faint hiss and pop of the candles.

Hugh took a deep breath and leaned forward. 'Did the abbot explain why I didn't ask you who attacked you on that fateful day?'

'I already knew,' Galen said. Not that he could speak at the time he'd been disowned, nor for several weeks afterwards, but that was irrelevant.

'You knew?' Hugh said.

'You were the first to think it, but not the last.'

'Everyone here thought you were complicit too, yes I know. The abbot told me. But you can tell me who it was now.'

If he weren't so scared, Galen might have laughed at his father's words. He made it sound so easy.

'You won't like to hear it. I'm not even sure you'll believe me.'

'It's somebody I know?'

'Somebody you respect,' Galen said, and his stomach twisted so violently with nerves he feared he might throw up. 'Somebody you love. I couldn't have told you who it was when he attacked me, for I knew you'd never believe me, even if I swore it in an oath.'

'For God's sake, Galen, I can't take this suspense anymore. Tell me who it was!'

Galen's throat threatened to seize up. If he spoke now, there would be no going back.

'It was Septimus,' Galen said, his voice coming out as a croak as he gathered his courage and looked his father in the eye.

'No!' Hugh said, recoiling. 'That can't be!'

Galen just watched his father, holding his breath, waiting to see what he would do next.

'You have to be lying.'

'What cause would I have to lie?'

'What cause? Septimus is my closest friend. He has stood beside me in battle since I was a boy. I love him. You are right. I love him more than you, and I love him more than I should love my wife. He has seen me through engagements far too numerous to mention. He has carried me from the battlefield when I was too injured to drag myself out. I would surely have died a hundred times if he hadn't come to my aid. How can I weigh up your words against his actions and accept what you are telling me?'

'Because it's the truth,' Galen said. It sounded inadequate, even to him.

'No!' a harsh voice shouted, and the denial rang through the church.

It was a voice Galen had prayed he'd never hear again. Septimus stalked out of the gloom, a dagger in his right hand. Galen gasped as he threw himself backwards and scrambled towards the altar as Septimus leaped up the steps, grabbed Galen by the front of his habit with his left hand and hoisted him off his feet.

'Recant,' Septimus hissed.

It tipped Galen straight back into his nightmare of helplessness. Septimus was three times his weight and towered over him. The arm that held Galen clear off the ground was the size of a tree trunk, roped with thick veins and rippling with muscle.

'When you attacked me,' Galen said, his words coming fast because he didn't have much time left, 'I bit your neck and tore off part of your right ear. How did you explain that away?'

'He knew I wouldn't even question him,' Hugh said as he stepped up behind Septimus. 'I would never have linked your attack with any injury to him.'

'I didn't do it!' Septimus shouted, as spit speckled his lips and hit Galen in the face.

'I might have believed you if you hadn't appeared here, Septimus,' Hugh said, reaching behind his back. 'I ordered all of you to stay in your quarters.'

'I had to know what he'd say. He was ever a cunning, lying creature,' Septimus said.

'Now there you are wrong. I never gave Galen credit for much, but I always took him for an honest boy. Maybe that was why I was so shocked when I saw him in that state and concluded what I did.'

'It's a lie!' Septimus growled.

At least this time Septimus was only holding on to his clothes. Galen tried to struggle free as he reached for the penknife tucked into his sleeve.

There was a second of telltale tensing, and Septimus stabbed at Galen. Hugh lunged forward and stabbed Septimus in the back with his right hand as he reached for Septimus's dagger with his left. His fingers tightened around the man's wrist. Galen stabbed low, aiming for the man's softest parts. Septimus screamed and dropped Galen and his dagger. Galen fell backwards and the full weight of Septimus landed on top of him, crushing the breath out of him.

Hugh grabbed the back of Septimus's collar and pulled him off Galen, who stared back at him, his small, bloody knife still clutched in his hand.

'You stabbed him?' Hugh said in surprise.

The knife fell out of Galen's suddenly nerveless fingers and he dragged himself backwards, twitching in pain and agitation as he slid across the floor, his hands first roaming to clutch his head and then jerking aimlessly about him.

Septimus's screams lowered to a faint groan as Hugh pulled him to his feet and locked his arm against the man's throat.

'Hold!' the abbot roared from the doorway. 'I will have no fighting in my church.'

Hugh swung round, hanging onto Septimus who was making a feeble attempt to break free.

'This is the man I came to unmask. I hope he didn't hurt anyone when he came into the church.'

'My people didn't see him. He must have slipped in through a side door, although I thought I had locked them.'

'Let me go, Hugh,' Septimus said through clenched teeth. 'You know what they will do to the likes of me.'

Galen remained on the floor. He had tried to push himself up onto his feet but couldn't. He prayed his father wouldn't be swayed by Septimus, even if they were closer than brothers.

'How can I let you go after what you have done, Septimus?' Hugh said. 'How could you betray me the way you did?'

'I love you,' Septimus said. 'I wanted you, not any of those other boys. But Galen was there, and he looked like you, and I couldn't resist. I couldn't hold myself back anymore.'

'You're sick!' Hugh said, his face twisted in revulsion.

'Then kill me. You owe me that at least, after all the times I've stood by you and protected you.'

'Stay your hand,' Dyrewine shouted as he saw Hugh tense. 'I will have no killings in the house of God.'

Hugh looked from the abbot to Galen. It surprised him that his father appeared to be asking him what to do, or at least giving him a say. Galen shook his head. Like the abbot, he couldn't allow Septimus to be killed in the church.

Hugh nodded grim acceptance and turned back to his erstwhile bosom companion.

'You will face justice for what you have done, Septimus. And I will sit through it all and accept blame for my part in the horror you perpetrated.'

The monks closed about Septimus to take him into custody and Hugh said, 'He was stabbed, once in the front and once in the back. His armour ensured my dagger did little harm, but you will still need to see to his wounds.'

'We will,' Abbot Dyrewine said, as he made to follow his monks out again.

He looked back at Hugh and then his gaze travelled to Galen who was watching them both.

Hugh turned to his son and asked, 'Are you alright?'

Galen nodded.

'I was certain he stabbed you.'

Galen had felt the tear of the dagger and now pulled his robe out to the side, inspecting a rent that went right through it.

'You put off his aim.'

'And you stabbed him. I wouldn't have thought it possible.' Galen nodded, not at all surprised by his father's reaction.

'Have I misjudged you all your life, Galen?'

Galen shrugged. Right now, all he wanted was to get up and away from here, but he could do neither. His heart jumped with fright as he heard someone else running towards them. What was it now? Had Septimus broken free?

'Galen, are you alright?' Alcuin said, emerging from the shadows.

Galen had never been more relieved to see anyone in his life. Alcuin would know what to do.

'I'm sorry, Galen, I swore you'd come to no harm and then that damned thane got in. He forced one of the side doors and none of us saw it.'

'I'm alright,' Galen murmured.

'Do you need help?'

Galen felt a flush of embarrassment suffuse his face to have this question asked in front of his father. Still, he couldn't get up without help, so he gave a slight nod and made sure not to make eye contact with Hugh.

He wondered why his father hadn't left already. After all, his business was complete. He'd do better to be watching Septimus, but he didn't move. Galen could feel they were being watched as Alcuin carefully helped him to his feet. Galen desperately wanted to stand up straight, now more than ever, but he couldn't. In fact, the pain was so great his legs were shaking. He took a couple of steps into the church, groped for the back of the chair Hugh had used and eased himself down onto it. Even with Alcuin's help he could get no further, as sweat beaded on his brow and trickled down his temple.

'Are you sure Septimus didn't get you?' Hugh said in a sharp voice. 'You look as pale as if you've been bled.'

Galen didn't know what to say in reply and gave up trying to look as if he were alright as he wrapped his arms tightly around his body.

'We need to get you to Brother Benesing, don't we?' Alcuin said so only Galen could hear him as he leaned down, examining Galen closely.

'Is this a friend of yours?' Hugh said from behind him.

'This is the great illuminator, Alcuin of Maccus,' Galen managed to say, although he spoke slowly, each word taking effort.

'Maccus!' Hugh shouted.

'Indeed. You need no introduction, my lord,' Alcuin said on a stiff bow.

'I dare say,' Hugh said. 'News of my name and my mission must have got round the abbey faster than fire, considering how quickly Galen hid away.'

'We all saw you arrive.'

Alcuin sounded defensive, and Galen could see that Hugh didn't like his tone. He was in no fit state to intercede and protect Alcuin. That thought would have amused him, but a wave of intense pain caused him to double over with a groan.

'Galen, what's wrong?'

'I've started to bleed.' The urgent need to get treated banished Galen's embarrassment to say such a thing before his father. 'I was shaken about rather a lot.'

'I'll take you to Brother Benesing,' Alcuin said, and helped to lift him from the pew.

It took all Galen's remaining reserves to stand, and he doubted he could take another step. In fact, he was seconds away from blacking out.

'What's wrong?' Hugh said.

'I'm sure Brother Benesing will explain,' Alcuin said, as he wrapped a sturdy arm around Galen's waist and lifted him so he took most of his weight.

'You need help,' Hugh said, as he took up position on Galen's other side.

He wrapped his arm so tightly about Galen's waist that it forced a gasp out of him.

'Gently, my lord!' Alcuin said. 'Else you'll do Galen an injury.'

'Are you sure Septimus's dagger missed you?' Hugh said.

'It did,' Galen said between high, fast breaths. 'It wasn't... his dagger that caused this injury.'

Hugh's lips closed tight on any further questions. He looked like he didn't want to hear more, which was a relief to Galen.

The journey to his uncle's house was a slow one and Galen would have been deeply ashamed that his father was having to do this if it weren't for the fact that he was in such pain it robbed him of the ability to worry about anything else.

'Wouldn't it be easier if I carried you?' Hugh said.

'No!' Galen said sharply. 'Please don't try.'

'I won't do anything you don't want,' Hugh said, much to Galen's relief. He could only imagine how bad the damage would be if he were run, shaken on every step, in Hugh's arms. Still, it was a nightmare walk through the night, down the barely visible path until they came to Benesing's screeching gate.

The cottage was in darkness when they arrived and Alcuin said, 'He's probably still at the infirmary.'

He tried the cottage door which, thankfully, swung open. The fire was lit and burning brightly, which made navigation to the cot Galen always occupied that much easier.

'You sit here,' Alcuin said, lowering Galen and indicating with his head for Hugh to do the same. 'I'll fetch Brother Benesing. My lord, if you wouldn't mind staying–'

'I'm not going anywhere,' Hugh snapped, which surprised Galen.

He glanced up at his father who was standing by his side, a fierce, unreadable scowl on his face as he watched Alcuin leave. It was a struggle for Galen to remain upright, but he would have been humiliated even more before his father if he had crumpled onto the cot. So, despite it costing him so much effort that all his muscles shook, he fought to stay alert and seated.

Although it was only a few minutes, it felt like an eternity until the familiar sound of the gate was heard and Benesing arrived.

He froze in his doorway as he spotted Hugh, and so was nearly run into by Alcuin, who had followed him.

'Ah,' he said.

'Hello Benesing,' Hugh said, looking the man over coolly. 'What have you been up to?'

'Patching up your thane,' Benesing said, as he moved to his cupboard of medicines and pulled out a clear syrup. Even though Galen knew what he would do, it still came as a relief to see him mix the medicine into a glass of water, turning it milky.

Benesing held the cup to Galen's lips. 'Alcuin said you've started to bleed again.'

Galen nodded and drank down the drug, grateful that they had finally reached this point.

'Alright, I will lie you down. Alcuin will help; he knows what to do so as not to hurt you.'

Galen wished with all his heart that his father wasn't still standing there, observing how pitiful his son was.

'God's tongue!' Hugh gasped and pointed at a patch of blood on the blanket where Galen had been sitting.

Benesing ignored his surprise and said, 'You'd better run along, Alcuin, it's nearly time for Compline.'

'Yes, Brother, I'm on my way. I'll drop in again this evening.'

Alcuin nodded a farewell to Galen, who managed a slight smile of thanks in reply. Then Alcuin bowed to Hugh and hurried away.

Benesing straightened up from Galen's side and looked Hugh over before he said, 'So, you've finally seen fit to find the man who injured Galen so grievously.'

'As you know,' Hugh said. 'Will Septimus live?'

The pain would ease soon and then Galen would slip into

oblivion, but he tried to hold off the stupor to hear the reply. It was important to him.

'You only got him a glancing blow and Galen stabbed him in the pudenda,' Benesing said. 'It was that which felled him, but it is by no means fatal. I've bandaged up the wounds and he'll heal quickly enough. What I want to know is what you will do with him now.'

'He will stand trial for sodomy and murder. Then we will execute him,' Hugh said. 'What's wrong with Galen?'

Galen's gaze was blurring, and the sound of his father's voice grew more distant. It was a curious effect of the drug his uncle administered that it could remove all feeling, not just the physical. So he wasn't as wracked with shame by his father's question, nor his uncle's reply, as he would normally be.

'The injuries Septimus inflicted upon him seem to be of a permanent nature. If he isn't careful, whatever healing has occurred gets ripped apart again and he starts to bleed.'

'What do you mean by careful?'

'No sudden movements and no jerking about. He can barely walk, he can't run and riding is out of the question.'

'And you can't heal him?'

'I haven't managed yet. Not that it's your problem and I dare say you'll want to be on your way,' Benesing said, by way of dismissal.

'So you will throw that in my face too, will you?' Hugh said.

'You disowned him. He is no better than a stranger to you. In fact,' Benesing said musingly, 'he was ever a stranger to you.'

'He was,' Hugh said. 'But I'll not be got rid of that easily.'

Galen had only a moment to wonder what his father meant before the medicine took full hold and sleep overwhelmed him.

Chapter 17

Galen sat up on his uncle's bed and looked about himself. He was alone. It was a cold, grey day that made him shiver and pull the blankets tighter about his shoulders, despite his uncle's perpetually burning fire.

Galen's mind was in turmoil and he couldn't understand why. He should have felt more at peace. His father had come and hadn't been the monster he'd grown into in Galen's mind. More importantly, Septimus had been unmasked.

Galen had never believed that Septimus would be brought to justice. The thought that the man who'd destroyed his life lived a life of honour and comfort with his father had always been a bitter burden for Galen to bear. But here they were now, Septimus under arrest and certain to be executed.

But instead of the overwhelming sense of satisfaction he should have expected, Galen felt hollow and sick. Maybe, somewhere in the back of his mind, he'd believed that if only Septimus were brought to justice, it would make everything right.

What a foolish wish. More a dream than anything else. Now, in the harsh light of day, so painfully, obviously, not true.

The signalling squeak of the gate shook Galen out of his introspection. It was probably his uncle, so Galen did no more than make sure his habit was in order.

'I see you're up,' Alcuin said, grinning at him as he stepped into the hut.

'Alcuin!'

He would know how to cheer Galen up and, at the very least, distract him for a while.

'Your uncle said you were well enough to see me,' Alcuin said, as he settled on the low stool beside him.

He had a gathering in his hands that filled Galen with anticipation.

'Is this our final chapter?'

'The second to last. This is where the paralysed man slept with the shoes of Saint Cuthbert on his feet and could walk again come morning.'

'Ah yes.'

Galen ran his finger gently over Alcuin's opening illustration. He'd drawn a picture of the saint holding his shoes out before him. All around Cuthbert, Alcuin had built up the parchment with gesso, covered the raised area with gold leaf and then etched an intricate pattern into the gold. Galen could feel the ripple of the shapes under his fingertip. If he held the image up to the light and tilted it back and forth, the pattern would appear and disappear depending on the angle, although the glow of the gold never lost its brilliance.

'It's beautiful,' Galen said. 'You have a remarkable talent.'

'No greater than yours,' Alcuin said.

Galen felt like he might puff out with pride every time Alcuin praised him. Since pride was a sin, he had to battle against it.

To distract himself, he said, 'I assume my father and his entourage have left.'

'Not yet,' Alcuin said. 'Although that blackguard Septimus was well enough to leave the infirmary three days ago. He's locked in a cell, so you don't have to worry about that.'

'How odd.' Galen was alarmed to hear that Septimus was still at the abbey, but trying hard not to let that show. 'I wonder why Ealdorman Hugh hasn't left yet?' It felt strange to call his father by his name, but Galen had little choice since he'd been disowned.

'You could always ask me yourself,' Hugh said, as he stepped into the cottage.

Galen got such a fright that he felt his stomach turn over in sick dread, and his left hand clenched so tight that his nail ripped through the leather and buried itself in his flesh. He'd been so distracted by his conversation with Alcuin that he hadn't even heard the gate. Now he was sitting in bed, at a distinct disadvantage, with his father towering over him.

Alcuin had also leapt to his feet. He took the gathering out of Galen's hand and said, 'I'd best be going. See you later.' He bowed stiffly to Hugh and hurried away.

Hugh grunted a farewell and then turned back to examining his son. Galen expected his father to react the way he always did, which, at best, was to shout at him to show some backbone and, at worst, to give him a disgusted look. Today there was something verging on sorrow in his eyes that

Galen had never seen.

Hugh sat down opposite Galen and said, 'Your uncle told me you were well enough to see me.'

'Yes.'

Galen squirmed under his father's searching gaze and wished he could meet him stare for stare.

'And your abbot gave me this codex to show me what you can do,' Hugh said, holding out the book of hours Galen had been working on before Alcuin had arrived at the abbey. It was now bound with a dark brown leather cover into which a geometric plait had been tooled.

'The abbot gave you a book?' Galen said, and his surprise deepened. It wasn't usual for the abbot to give out gifts unless he expected something in return. And it was Hugh who owed the abbot for allowing him in and resolving his problem, not the other way around.

'It's a gift of great value,' Hugh said, turning the book over in his hands and rubbing the cover with his fingertips. 'I doubt I've ever seen a codex as fine as this before.'

Galen blinked in surprise at his father and wished he could be more worthy of him. Instead, he was bent over in a bed. Could he look any more miserable?

Hugh reached across the gap between them, grabbed Galen's left hand and eased it open.

'No,' Galen said, and pulled his hand away.

'You've cut yourself,' Hugh said.

Galen nodded. What more could he do?

'I didn't realise that was why you wore that glove. I thought it had something to do with being a scribe.'

'Have you ever seen a scribe wearing a leather glove?'

'What do I know of scribes? I dare say it's useful to have gloves when it's cold so you can still do the fine work you need to do.'

'Woollen ones,' Galen murmured.

Hugh nodded, then his eyes dropped back to the codex. It was so unusual for Hugh not to hold somebody's gaze that Galen wondered what on earth was going on.

'Do you want to be a monk, Galen?'

'What else could I be?' Galen said, back to being wary. Where was his father going with this line of questioning?

Hugh shrugged and said, 'I don't know. I dare say I could find something for you to do on my estates.'

Galen couldn't help but stare at his father, as though he'd turned into some fantastical beast.

This got a wry laugh from the man. 'Does it surprise you that much?'

Galen nodded, so astonished that he didn't even look away.

'I always thought of becoming a monk. I'm shy, I find it uncomfortable being amongst people I don't know, and I don't have the heart or the build to be a warrior. The only other option I could see was to be a monk. Which was why I applied myself to my studies.'

'Did you?' Hugh said. 'I didn't notice.'

'No,' Galen said softly. He knew it for a fact.

'But what of women, Galen? Did you never think you'd like to get married? Was there no woman who attracted your notice?'

'Cwengyth, but she never had eyes for anyone but Willnoth,' Galen said with a wistful sigh. He wondered why he was being so open with his father. This whole situation was so strange. They'd never had a conversation before, and now... to be having that most manly of chats. Galen had always burned with embarrassment when he overheard talk about women amongst the men in his father's hall.

'Cwengyth!' Hugh said with a laugh. 'Well, she's married to Fulk now that he's my heir.'

Galen nodded.

'There was no-one else?' Hugh asked.

'Not really. I worked myself into an agony of embarrassment whenever I contemplated talking to any beauty. And now...' Galen flushed and said, 'I can't. I might cause myself an injury if I tried to bed a woman. The pain also takes away any appetite I may have had for it, which is just as well, as I've taken a vow of celibacy.'

'So I can't talk you into leaving?'

'Why would you want to?' Galen was getting steadily more confused.

His father looked strangely uncomfortable too. He leaped to his feet and made a circuit of the hut, his head brushing against the herbs that hung from Benesing's roof.

'It isn't like these monks have treated you well, is it? I've been told you are ostracised.'

'Perhaps that will change now. Besides, I've got used to it.'

'What if it doesn't change? Surely you would be better off at home?'

'At home?' Galen really couldn't understand what his father was trying to say. He felt as if he was missing some important piece of this puzzle. 'You threw me out. You disowned me.'

'What I did was wrong. I wish I could take it all back. I

wish I had sought justice for you from the moment we found you.'

Galen stared at his father, terrified that he was mistaken in what he was trying to say. He didn't dare reply in case he was wrong.

Hugh gave an uncomfortable laugh and said, 'I'm trying to apologise, Galen. I'm asking for your forgiveness. If you can see your way to accepting it, I'd like to take you back as my son.'

'Oh.'

'Is that all you have to say?' Hugh said. 'Galen? Are you alright?'

'I don't think so,' Galen said faintly, and swayed in his seat.

He barely understood what his father had just said because it was so unlikely to come from him. He wanted to burst into tears of relief. It left him immobilised.

'Galen!' Hugh said, and grabbed his arms to steady him. 'Should I call your uncle?'

'No, I'll be alright,' Galen said, trying hard not to let his tumultuous emotions show.

'Did I give you such a shock with my apology?'

'I think you must have.'

'Can you forgive me?'

'Yes.'

It was so easy for Galen to say it. He felt it should have been harder. He should have fought against it, but he couldn't.

'Can you find it in your heart to accept me back as your father?'

Galen nodded, ashamed that he was so happy, and feeling

odd to see his father looking so awkward.

'But you'll stay here?'

'I think so... My uncle is close at hand to keep me alive,' Galen said, wondering whether he'd somehow slipped into one of those disturbingly real dreams his uncle's medicine induced.

'I see,' Hugh said. 'I suppose then it's wisest you stay. But if you ever change your mind, send me word and I'll help you go somewhere else. Your uncle tells me you can't ride, but I can send a cart for you.'

'Thank you,' Galen said, and looked up at his father. He seemed like a stranger, this man who showed so much understanding.

Hugh gave a rueful smile and said, 'You're finding this strange.'

'Yes.' Galen could hardly deny it.

'I'm sorry. I've just realised that my current consideration is beyond anything you've experienced from me. I'm ashamed that my friends and your brothers are familiar with how far I'm willing to go for any of them. It hurts me now that I've never done the same for you.'

Galen felt his face flush to hot, prickling shame and muttered, 'It's alright.'

'Mmm,' Hugh grunted. 'I think I'll give this book of hours to your mother as a gift from you. If you like, I'll convey a letter to her from you too.'

'A letter from me?' Galen said, relieved to be onto safer ground, and happier than he could tell his father over the offer to send a letter to his mother.

'Certainly. You asked if she'd sent a message for you, so I

assume you want to hear from her.'

'Yes.'

'But you've never written to her?'

'I didn't dare. I feared she might not write back, or write and tell me to leave her alone.'

'After she saved your life?'

'That was different. She might still not want to hear from me.'

'She misses you,' Hugh said. 'You were ever one of her favourites.'

'Do you think so?' So far Galen hoped he'd hidden his own emotions, his hurt, reasonably well. He'd been surprised, even shocked, but he hadn't allowed his father to see his pain. Now he feared, judging by the contrite expression on his father's face, that he'd betrayed himself again.

'I know she misses you,' Hugh said. 'I'm sorry, you must have been very lonely. But, never fear, I'm certain that once she gets a letter from you, she'll write back.'

'When are you going?' Galen said, and felt stupid and embarrassed to make it sound like he was eager for his father to leave.

'As soon as I have your letter. I've been kicking my heels for long enough in this place. It's time I was heading home.'

Chapter 13

lcuin was unsurprised to find Galen seated on the bench in his uncle's herb garden. Although winter was nearly upon them, they did still get the occasional sunny day. Galen was taking advantage of it and soaking in the sun. He had his head tilted upwards and his eyes closed. Unusually for him, he had a slight smile playing on his lips. The letter clasped loosely on his lap explained that.

Alcuin sat down next to him and also turned his face up into the watery sunshine.

'I do like it when the sun's warmth lingers. There's nothing like sunshine soaking into these black robes for warming a body up.'

Galen opened his eyes and sat forward. 'I know it heralds winter. But I have always liked autumn. It is a pleasant time of the year.'

'And it provides a rich bounty in fruit and vegetables, which I always like.' Alcuin tilted his chin down at Galen's hands and said, 'Is that a letter from home?'

'My mother has written.'

'I thought it must be something important, the way you slipped off in the middle of Anfred's riveting dissertation on the signs to be read everywhere of the coming apocalypse. Honestly, the man is obsessed, but I had no idea he had drawn up such a comprehensive list.'

'There's no arguing with Anfred,' Galen said, his elusive smile touching his lips.

'You don't try to at any rate. I'm more foolish. I leaped in.'

Galen gave a slight nod.

Alcuin examined his face again. It was still pale, but more at peace now that his name had been cleared. While his acceptance into the brotherhood was slow, the others were gradually warming to Galen.

He was still painfully shy, and far too insecure to push himself into their society, but he drew nearer these days when they held their discourses. Once, he'd even offered his opinion. It was well reasoned, which surprised everyone but Alcuin. And better yet, he'd not been shut out when he'd ventured his mild interjection, which had encouraged Galen all the more.

'Is the news from home good?'

'Very,' Galen said. 'My mother sent a great deal of gossip, all about herself and the burh and what my sisters are up to.'

Alcuin had never seen Galen look so animated as now. It reminded him of what Brother Benesing had said, that he'd had a spark of life that was charming. Now, as he poured out the details of his sisters' plans, which mostly consisted of whom they would marry, he really came alive.

'My mother also sends her love to me and her thanks to

you,' Galen finished, with a shy flush suffusing his face.

'Thanks to me?!' Alcuin said, with a surprised laugh. 'What on earth for?'

'For being a friend to me.'

'How could I not be? I need to keep on the good side of a scribe who makes my illuminations look so much better than they deserve.'

'A very good friend,' Galen said, with a warm smile, 'and I thank you for it, Alcuin.'

Enjoyed this book?

If you are like me, you use reviews to decide whether you want to buy a book. So if you enjoyed the book please take a moment to let people know why. The review can be as short as you like.

Thank you very much!

https://www.amazon.com/review/create-review

Offer

Get a free eBook - Sanctuary
Plus exclusive, behind the scenes, material

Building a relationship with my readers is one of the great things about being a writer. Sign up for my no-spam newsletter that only goes out when there is a new book or freebie available.

You can sign up and get a free eBook of my medieval mystery romance, Sanctuary, at: www.marinapacheco.me

About the Author

Marina Pacheco is a travelling author who currently lives in Lisbon, after stints in London, Johannesburg and Bangkok. She is an introvert who writes feel-good novels that are perfect to curl up with on a rainy day. Her books often have a strong romantic element where good triumphs over evil and the girl gets the boy in the end.

Online home: https://marinapacheco.me

Facebook: https://www.facebook.com/100bookschallenge/

Amazon Author Page: https://www.amazon.co.uk/Marina-Pacheco/e/B07D5H2PDG/ref=dp_byline_cont_ebooks_1

email: marina.pacheco@gmail.com

Books by Marina Pacheco

Historical Romance

Sanctuary – free ebook – available here: https://geni.us/cgXO He needs shelter. She wants a way out. Will his brave move to protect risk both their hearts? If you like optimistic tales of redemption, heart-warming characters, and feel-good thrills, then you'll adore Marina Pacheco's historical tale.

The Duke's Heart – available here: https://geni.us/PTconXt His body may be weak, but his dreams know no bounds. Will she be the answer to his prayers? If you like unique leading men, strong and determined women, and slow-build relationships, then you'll adore Marina Pacheco's delightful courtship.

Duchess in Flight – available here: https://geni.us/mKyNY7 She's on the run from a deadly enemy. He lives in the shadows of truth. When their lives merge, will their battle for survival lead to love? If you like reluctant heroes, strong women, and chances for redemption, then you'll adore Marina Pacheco's adventurous tale.

Medieval Historical Fiction

Life of Galen Series

Fraternity of Brothers – Life of Galen, Book 1 – available here: https://geni.us/U6ny8 Cast out for a crime committed against him, his future looks bleak. Until an unexpected visitor gives him hope for justice. If you like fighting for acceptance, finding absolution, and authentic depictions of the harsh Middle Ages, then you'll love Marina Pacheco's riveting novella.

Comfort of Home – Life of Galen, Book 2 – available here: https://geni.us/0c65yv Proven innocent, he's returned from exile. Can he recover all that he lost? If you like captivating characters, chances for redemption, and uplifting quests, then you'll love Marina Pacheco's immersive tale.

Kindness of Strangers – Life of Galen, Book 3 – available here: https://geni.us/7AP7 Trapped in a land plagued by vikings, can one small miracle be all they need to survive? If you like historical detail, human dilemmas, and a heartwarming story, then you'll love Marina Pacheco's absorbing tale.

Coming Soon

Restless Sea – Life of Galen, Book 5
Friend of my Enemy – Life of Galen, Book 6
Road to Rome – Life of Galen, Book 7
Eternal City – Life of Galen, Book 8
Love and Loss – Life of Galen, Book 9
Return of the Wanderers – Life of Galen, Book 10

Science Fiction / Fantasy

City of Night – Eternal City, Book 1 – available here: https://geni.us/BYHxkAT They come from opposite ends of the city, but it might as well be different worlds. Will a demon threat be what's needed to bring them together? City of Night is a futuristic urban sci-fi/ fantasy with a satisfying ending. If you enjoy odd couples, mysteries and unusual settings, then you'll love the unique world Marina Pacheco has created.

Acknowledgements

Although writing is a solitary exercise, it is enhanced by the support and enthusiasm of friends, family and a team of professionals who have all encouraged me to keep going at various points in my life.

Special thanks to:

My beta readers, who send back really helpful suggestions that improve the story.

My street team, who let the world know about my books.

My editor, Katharine D'Souza Editorial Services: http://www.katharinedsouza.co.uk, who significantly improves on all my stories.

My proofreader, Candida Burrows, who picks up more mistakes than I care to admit to. You can contact her at: candidaburrows47@gmail.com

100 Covers for their patience and understanding and fantastic covers.

All I can say is thank you and let's do it all again!!

* * *

Printed in Great Britain
by Amazon

87762922R00109